A Prayer For
Katerina Horovitzova

Also by Arnošt Lustig, published by Quartet Books

Darkness Casts No Shadow
Diamonds of the Night
Night and Hope

A Prayer For
Katerina Horovitzova

Arnošt Lustig

Translated by Jeanne Němcová

Quartet Books

Published in Great Britain by Quartet Books Limited 1990
A member of the Namara Group
27/29 Goodge Street
London W1P 1FD

A catalogue record for this title is available from the British Library

Printed and bound in Great Britain
at The Camelot Press, Trowbridge, Wiltshire.

ONE

Mr. HERMAN COHEN, equipped with an American passport like the other nineteen men in the low-ceilinged synagogue, had asked Mr. Brenske to find him a tailor, and when the tailor came, he said, "I want you to make me a traveling suit to replace the one I'm wearing now. It's almost worn out, you see. I want you to do the best job you can and make me something with a lot of style. I'll see you're well paid for it."

He said it just as though he were in San Francisco. He didn't let himself be disturbed by the presence of the soldier who had brought the tailor from the adjacent camp, or by the guards in the corners of the synagogue.

For more than an hour and a half, the synagogue and its outbuildings had been guarded inside and out by soldiers dressed like this one, in the same frog-green uniform, the color of oozy mud and water lily pads. It was on the loading ramp at the station that Katerina Horovitzova, contradicting her father for the first time in her life, had said, "But I don't want to die. . . ." This was what had first aroused

Mr. Cohen's admiration and made him intercede for her with Mr. Brenske right there at the railroad siding. It had acted on her like a sweet and heavy wine which makes you dizzy in a strange, deep, blissful way. That's how she imagined wine would make her feel, although she had never tasted a drop of it. She did not know then that by the very act of interceding on her behalf, Mr. Herman Cohen was trying to find out whether Mr. Friedrich Brenske's intentions toward them were honest or not. Which was why he'd asked for a tailor too. By the way he'd said at first, "I want you to make me a traveling suit . . ." he demonstrated his confidence that everything was quite natural. According to Mr. Brenske, the man had until not long ago been the best tailor in Warsaw.

"I want a suit," Mr. Herman Cohen went on in a kindly, casual tone, addressing the tailor in his striped prison uniform and the soldier too who stood at his elbow, as if the tailor might be armed or liable to commit all sorts of wickedness. "I want a suit with the right amount of tucks in the right places so it won't wrinkle and it won't rip. You know what I mean, I'm sure. A stylish cut, naturally, and I'd prefer a dark material: it makes you look slimmer. But on the other hand, I don't want black either, as though I were in mourning. Now, for Miss Horovitzova here, whom I'm going to look after from now on as if she were my own flesh and blood, I want you to whip up a suit and coat that'll keep her warm in this miserable weather, but something she can wear and not be ashamed of out in the world. I probably don't have to tell you," he added, using the same tone he had adopted when he had first addressed the tailor, "that I want nothing but the best for me and for her and that money is no object."

4

He had spoken this way only to give himself courage, because the tailor was listening apathetically, ready to do the best he could under any circumstances. As he was speaking, Mr. Cohen kept puzzling over why the people on the ramp had been whispering about some gas "in there." What kind of gas do you suppose they meant?

Katerina Horovitzova ran her hands along her hips unconsciously, as though she were about to try on the new suit. She still hadn't quite absorbed how all this had happened, but now she was concentrating on immediate needs. She was prepared to act the part of an experienced and famous dancer as she had at first when she had been left alone for a few moments with Mr. Herman Cohen. That was when he had told her that this wasn't so important right now, and that for the moment she shouldn't worry about what would become of her afterward, that there wouldn't be any problem; one of the other gentlemen, Mr. Rappaport-Lieben from Chicago, held a lot of shares in the stockyards and he also owned a big nightclub, the Gondola. She remembered the name. Too bad there hadn't been time for him to tell her more about it. But then Mr. Brenske and the other guards came back and she said no more.

Apparently the gentlemen with the American passports had not known each other very well before. There had been two thousand of them to start with, not just twenty, but (and this they had been told in Italy, which is where they had come from) the competent American authorities were mainly interested in these twenty wealthy gentlemen. The German side wasn't much interested either in anonymous, rank-and-file German soldiers; what they cared about was a certain general and other high-ranking officers. So in view of these gentlemen's great wealth on one hand and the general's importance on the other, everything that had happened up to now had been quite extraordinary.

The tailor was as skinny as his shadow and he had a bruise on his forehead. He was trembling, perhaps with a scorn he had learned to hide during the years he'd spent in the camp next door, so no one could tell whom he held to blame for the wrongs which had been done to him. He kept staring inoffensively but steadily at the hulking shoulders of Herman Cohen, who was beginning to show signs of stoutness. He was rich, you could tell that at a glance, and from the way he talked when he was ordering the suit, he must be a millionaire many times over.

To the others who were standing around, the tailor's expression might have been disguising the calculating yet stern vigilance of a master craftsman who was reluctant to admit his new role. There was also a penetrating inquisitiveness in the way he looked, together with the sadness of someone who shrewdly suspects that those shoulder pads which he was staring at were stuffed with gold and foreign currency. Finally, he was probably envious. What if the suit which he was going to make for Mr. Cohen really would be worn by him when he left this place?

Thousands, even hundreds of thousands, no, millions of people, the tailor thought to himself, would have narrowed down their most fervent wishes to just one thing: to be able to leave this camp. As though in itself this would have meant the beginning of a better life. And suddenly, right here in front of him, stood two flesh-and-blood examples of people who were going to leave: Mr. Herman Cohen and Katerina Horovitzova.

Despite the uniformed guards and the wires charged with deadly electricity and despite the concrete walls which

6

made the camp an almost impregnable fortress, everybody knew by now that there was this group of twenty American Jews in the nearby synagogue, most of them originally from Poland. A few were apparently from Bohemia. It was already an open secret that they had been taken prisoner during the Allied landings in Sicily after the German Army had occupied most of the country, including Rome. And now these twenty Americans had been brought here. After a brief wait on the ramp, they were taken in charge by Mr. Friedrich Brenske, commandant of the camp's secret division, who immediately made sure that they were given special treatment. He assured them that they would be briefly interned in the old synagogue buildings until they were able to continue on their way to the west, away from the former Polish territory, now administered by the General Government. He also told them that he would personally make every effort to satisfy all their wishes provided, of course, that this was in his power and not contrary to the interests of the Reich because, even in such an exceptional case, it's still true that blood is thicker than water. This was probably overheard by some of the other people who had just come from Warsaw; they had arrived at the ramp aboard another train after blundering for days over the railroads of what had once been Poland. One of the new arrivals was Katerina Horovitzova. As her father looked out at all the people on the other side of the barbed wire and at the tall, smoldering smokestacks beyond the railroad tracks, he said, "We've come here to meet our death."

It wasn't considered polite to contradict Father in the Horovitz family, and anyway she wasn't independent enough for that yet, but she had been so exhausted and frightened when she got out of the train that she disagreed with her father, first inside herself and then out loud. It may have been the expression on her face or her dancer's grace, her dignity or maybe even an explicit plea—no one was quite sure and it didn't matter anyway in the end—which led Herman Cohen, as intermediary between the Americans and Mr. Brenske, to ask for her. That was just as she had been telling her father earnestly, "But I don't want to die. . . ." The whole camp knew by now that Mr. Brenske had agreed without a moment's hesitation. This fact, more than anything else he'd said or done, spread through the camp like wildfire. He told Katerina Horovitzova to step forward and join the Americans, adding that her luggage would be brought later. As soon as she moved out of the ranks, her father was jostled forward by the crowd. And in the same camp, just a few steps away, they even knew that right after that, Katerina Horovitzova's mother, her father, grandfather and all six sisters went into the gas chamber, just as she was leaving the ramp along with Mr. Brenske and the others. She kept turning around and trying to find her father in the turmoil between the railroad tracks and the path, but everybody had lost track of everybody else; they kept looking around for their luggage, wives searched for husbands, and fathers and mothers sought their children and vice versa. In the camp, people even knew that Katerina Horovitzova's family had been led into Gas Chamber 3 and that afterward, all nine bodies had been cremated in the oven supervised by Rabbi Dajem from Lodz.

The tailor watched Mr. Herman Cohen and out of the corner of his eye he watched the soldier too so he needn't look directly at Katerina Horovitzova. He didn't know how to tell her what had happened to her family or whether it was even a good idea for her to know about it. He could see from her childlike expression, her ripening body and face, that she really was just as they'd said she was in the camp. In little more than half an hour, Katerina Horovitzova had become a legend and everybody was talking about this beautiful but cowardly Jewish girl who had managed to escape the fate met by the rest of her family. It had been cowardice by necessity, but perhaps not entirely. After all, other people wanted to live too. As if they didn't know what was going to happen to them. Anyway, wasn't the whole outside world just like the camp by now, which stretched its barbed wire like greedy, brutal hands and which no one could escape? That was why at first the tailor had repudiated the Polish-American Herman Cohen, then changed his mind and forgiven him for the complacent tone he'd used in speaking to him. He was circumcised the same as he had been himself. To conceal his thoughts, he went on pretending to be interested in the rich man's shoulder pads. He was thinking about Katerina Horovitzova again, about the other things he'd heard from the lips of the older, more erudite prisoners with whom he associated and who had not yet been sent to the gas chambers. By now they were only a pitiful remnant because a strong body is more resistant for a longer time than a sturdy soul. They had been telling him legends of an ancient land where some famous young woman, with the help of her uncle, had been able to save her innocent brothers from extermination. There was a story too from medieval Spain in which a certain king in his passion forgot his own wife because of a lovely Jewish girl. Something of the exotic, quite unreal charm of these old legends lingered like an echo even now as some of their words came back to him. Thinking about her, it was as if this was a culmination, even though it was not quite certain how she would end up. But there was that clear understanding that it was all over now for the rest of her family. It had taken about an hour and a half, he thought to himself, and it had happened while he and Mr. Herman Cohen and the other nineteen American gentlemen and Katerina Horovitzova had been here, inhaling the muddy autumnal air of these Polish plains, air that was greasy with the stench of incinerated human bones and flesh and lard, which even overwhelmed the ancient smell of the marshes.

They had begun to talk about her in all the nooks and corners of the camp, how when she was only twelve she had preferred to dance instead of doing her lessons, about how often she'd been spanked because if a Jewish mother spares the rod, she really doesn't love her child. Then later, they said, after Colonel Beck's Poland had become the General Government, Katerina had apparently been dancing at a party when the Germans attacked; all the other girls and women had been raped, they said, all of them except her, because she had quite captivated the German commander, who afterward had been demoted because of it and immediately sent off to the Eastern Front, where he was shot, not by Russian snipers but by a German bullet from a Parabellum pistol used by the military police. Right through the back of the neck, the way a traitor dies. Rumors of her former glory raced ahead of reality and the people in the camp even described how she had danced on stages in what was for them the world—in a London music hall, for instance, and in San Francisco, where, someone said, Mr. Herman Cohen had gone after he'd left Warsaw. They'd also found out, only God knows how, that Mr. Rappaport-Lieben owned shares in the Chicago stockyards and that he was a well-known master of ceremonies at his nightclub, the

Gondola. So this man Cohen was different than they were, even though he too had been circumcised. He had another kind of passport, but this didn't really make such a difference. Actually, it was more of an invisible bond between them. The tailor stood there, his mind busy with all kinds of conjectures. The zebra-striped prison clothes draped into his sagging shoulders; the sleeves were too long. Maybe this was because of the hunched way he was standing and the carelessness of his posture, which showed he wasn't paying attention to how he looked but was immersed in his thoughts. Certainly this hardly could have inspired much confidence about his skill with needle and scissors in Mr. Cohen and Katerina Horovitzova. He didn't even have pins sticking out between his lips as real tailors usually do, or an oilcloth tape measure flung back around his neck; his long, skinny fingers were all that showed he'd done a lot of sewing. The index and middle fingers on his right hand were rough and discolored, as if he never used a thimble.

The corporal who had brought the tailor had obviously already reached the outward boundary of adolescence. He couldn't have been more than twenty-one, one of those fledgling German youngsters who had grown up there in the camp and with whom the tailor was familiar. Molded by the stern camp routine which applied to both sides, they either had to be unfeeling or else at night, on the other side of the barbed wire, they turned their guns against themselves, the barrel filled with water and the muzzle stuck into their mouths or under their chins. All they had to do was press the trigger with their toes. Some of them went crazy under pressure of the strange things they'd seen or else they were shot by their own comrades who had steeled themselves better to the job. The tailor had seen one such execu-

11

tion with his own eyes, performed by Lieutenant Horst Schillinger in front of the prisoners; it was an infantryman who couldn't stand watching little children and old people being burned, evidently forgetting that these people were not a chosen race and that he must not be found guilty of the sin of compassion. Apparently he had said he wanted to have nothing to do with the whole thing. The execution took place near the tailor shop and as Mr. Friedrich Brenske told Lieutenant Horst Schillinger at the time, it made its point for both sides. As a warning, the infantryman was cremated like a "white Jew," a defiler of the Nordic race, in the third oven, where Rabbi Dajem of Lodz held sway and where they dried the women's hair that had been sheared from the corpses as they came out of the gas chambers. But this was done only after it had been carefully rinsed, so the hair was damp but not dirty.

Rabbi Dajem of Lodz was Mr. Brenske's plaything. He sang beautifully, which was discovered accidentally. When the old man was being herded into a gas chamber, he had been trying unsuccessfully to cheer his dying brothers with song and Mr. Brenske had heard him through the door. He ordered it to be opened, had the old man dragged out and told him to sing that lovely song in the hair-drying room. From then on, that had been his job.

The fledgling corporal who had brought the tailor over from the camp was watching Katerina Horovitzova with calculating eyes. His name was Emerich Vogeltanz; the tailor had found that out when he had stitched up the sweatband in his cap where his name was stamped. It wasn't a compassionate look he gave her, but it was appreciative. A child and a woman both. Now the thing was, which of these aspects do you want to suppress and which bring to the fore? At that moment, the tailor and Mr. Herman Cohen both felt a single-minded pride, as though they had agreed on it in advance.

"What did you do before, cutie pie?" asked Corporal Vogeltanz.

"I was a dancer," she replied.

"Hmmm . . ."

Well, well, even the supermen admire this tender young Jewish flower and they show it too; the first chord of understanding was struck between the tailor and the rich man with his American passport as they exchanged a glance. The way the corporal had said, "Hmmm," and then his gesture, were enough for the glimmer in the tailor's eye to be reflected in the moisture which filmed Mr. Herman Cohen's small and watchful eyes. Both of them told themselves that Mr. Cohen had done a good deed in rescuing this girl from death. Even though Mr. Cohen was reluctant to think about the needlessly depressing notions which kept haunting him when he remembered what he had seen and heard on the loading ramp and when he looked at the pitiful hunched figure of the tailor, still the other gentlemen had begun to realize by now what the camp was all about. Nobody had needed to tell them. So in addition to the sincere pride and admiration which they shared, a signal passed from the brain of one man to that of the other. There was something the tailor knew but Mr. Herman Cohen didn't. Or maybe it was something he didn't want to think about. He waited patiently for the tailor's answer as he drew himself up a trifle straighter.

Katerina Horovitzova felt that everybody was looking at her and she reminded herself that she must behave with restraint, at least until they got out of this place, beyond the

boundaries of the camp and then beyond the boundaries of
the Reich itself. She wished she could force herself to stop
thinking about her youngest sister, Lea, and about her
mother. Whenever she thought of the two of them, she
always remembered the rest of her family too, and one by
one they passed through her mind. Nine people, not counting her. She had made up her mind to take advantage once
again of Mr. Herman Cohen's kindness and ask him to help
them too, even though Mr. Brenske had implied that for the
time being it was enough that one exception had been made
and she had been allowed to go with Mr. Cohen as his
companion. But Mr. Brenske hadn't actually said this in so
many words, either to her or to Mr. Cohen. That was why
she was waiting now for the moment when this whole crazy
business with the tailor and the clothes was over. When Mr.
Cohen had first asked to have a new suit made, Mr. Brenske
had arranged it very willingly, but at the same time he
explained that it would not be possible for all the other
gentlemen to have new suits made because there simply
wasn't enough time and not enough top-quality tailors for
so many people. Mr. Brenske even admitted that the rum-
pled suits of the other men, who had hardly slept a wink
during their trip from Italy, might perhaps cause some dis-
paraging remarks when they got to the place where they
were to be exchanged. But with a little bit of good will,
anybody would realize that this just proved that the Germans had been in a hurry. By that time, the gentlemen
would be glad to forget the fuss they'd made about their
clothes because they'd be shopping around for new suits.

"It's not much for the price," he said. "Let him who is
without fault throw the first stone."

Suddenly, Corporal Emerich Vogeltanz spat juicily onto

14

the floor right in the middle of the room where Mr. Herman Cohen stood. He did it so everybody could see. Maybe it was intended to disguise the admiration he had shown, for he kept on mumbling, "Hmmm . . ."

She really was damn good looking, this Jew bitch, Emerich Vogeltanz admitted to himself; well built, a bit taller than Herman Cohen, who wasn't such a runt himself, and she had narrow shoulders and a smooth, slender back. He observed the expression on her face, which was that of a startled, wary child, the corners of her mouth a trifle drooping. Her forehead was creased with a straight line, which was both sharp and gentle.

"I'll do my best," the tailor said, "so it's the way you want it. . . ."

The eyes of the sergeant, the tailor and Mr. Herman Cohen were all turned on the face and body of Katerina Horovitzova. Under different circumstances, this probably would have embarrassed her, but now all the ordinary circumstances were happening simultaneously. Causes and effects were all mixed up. Suddenly the attraction which they all felt was the only thing she had to hold onto. Her mother's old warnings and scoldings were out of place now; she must act a part. She knew it wasn't quite right, maybe, but it was the only way out. She mustn't hang onto a word like "right" or "wrong"—such words were beside the point now. And so she endured the way they were looking at her.

"Hm, hmmm . . ." mumbled Emerich Vogeltanz again. He couldn't think of anything more expressive.

Her legs were graceful as a doe's and her hair was black as the blackest coal, long, strong and glossy. Her eyes looked less melancholy now. They glistened like old copper, a mixture of brown and green with a gentle breath of gold.

"I'll do the best I can and as fast as possible," the tailor reassured them as he hunched his shoulders. He probably wanted to divert attention from the spitting incident.

But it was still in the air. It hadn't been erased or removed by what Herman Cohen had been saying before it happened, speaking like someone who is aware of his own importance. Even with the camp next door. Yes, I'll ask him, just as soon as we're alone, Katerina Horovitzova said to herself, with even more determination than at first. She would ask Mr. Herman Cohen to buy freedom for her mother and father and grandfather and for her six sisters. The words and phrases rushed together which she would use to plead her case. The soldier frightened her and even though they were silent, the other guards were frightening too. In such company, the tailor, by his mere physical presence, aroused a different kind of horror, even a revulsion, because he looked so miserable and because he reminded her of all the things she probably didn't want to see. All she wanted was for him to give a message to her family so they would know she was going to try to help them. Her thoughts kept going back to that moment when they were all together on the ramp and there on the next track came a diesel locomotive pushing an Italian railroad coach with these twenty distinguished gentlemen on board. Immediately hope kindled in her. They'd known where they were going as soon as they had reached the outskirts of Warsaw. There had been a lot of talk about the camp and a lot of silence too. All of it was true. When they arrived, a husky, dark-haired German officer with a mustache sent her mother and sisters off in one direction and then Father disappeared too. All she could do was try to send a message with Mrs. Mandelbaum who used to live on Low Street in Warsaw, saying that she was going to go with these American gentlemen. Mr. Herman Cohen had immediately agreed to pay the money Mr. Brenske asked for, because he'd overheard her saying, "But I don't want to die. . . ." He had grasped at the chance almost gratefully, because the trip from Italy had been dreary and depressing and he wanted to give some sort of hope to himself and to the other nineteen gentlemen. He knew how to take a chance. One of the others, probably Mr. Oscar Lowenstein, remarked that they would do better to simply look out for themselves, but there was another aspect to it—the feeling that they were still able to do something, individually or as a group, even in these surroundings and under such circumstances.

Mr. Brenske had said something about one hundred thousand gold Swiss francs. Katerina Horovitzova didn't blush or turn pale. She had stopped being surprised. She could hardly imagine so much money. Mr. Stepan Gerstl had stepped out on the ramp right after she'd been ransomed and had begun to tell everybody about a dream he'd had. He'd dreamed about a banquet, he said, and he didn't know what that was supposed to signify. This reminded the other gentlemen that it had been a long time since they had slept or eaten. But nobody made any comment. How could Mr. Gerstl have dreamed, when he hadn't been asleep? Or really awake either. If Mr. Herman Cohen would give the tailor some money now, she thought to herself, he might be more obliging and that would be one step forward. She was ashamed of herself for being so ready to spend Mr. Herman Cohen's money, but these were unusual circumstances, after all, and she was ready to do anything to repay him,

17

once they were across the border. But maybe he wasn't doing this for money at all. She'd lost sight of Mrs. Mandelbaum on the ramp. She had searched in vain for the outline of her head and shoulders while Mr. Brenske and Mr. Cohen were hurrying them along so they wouldn't blunder among the railroad sidings. Mr. Brenske kept reminding them that they must be careful not to catch some disease which might jeopardize their trip, because the other new arrivals had not yet been disinfected. When he said this, one of the gentlemen glanced quickly at Katerina Horovitzova and then the whole group moved on, escorted by Mr. Brenske and the rest of his men, to the empty synagogue.

It was probably true here too, she thought, as it was on both sides of the ghetto wall in Warsaw, that for foreign currency or gold you could always buy plenty of things from the German Army or from the secret police—things as precious as dark Polish or German army bread or cans of Portuguese sardines decorated with Salazar's picture. Not to mention such nonessential delicacies as well-cured smoked beef. In the Horovitz family they had always believed that the souls of birds and animals were concealed within their blood, so every meat dish was eaten only after its spiritualized blood had first been drained away. That had been once or maybe twice a week, if there was a holiday. Again thoughts of her youngest sister, Lea, rushed in. She mustn't be left behind in that camp! Once again Katerina reproached herself for having deserted her family. But the camp meant death and there might still be life wherever the camp didn't reach. She consoled herself that anybody else would have done the same if they had been in her place. But she could not get the vision of her little sister out of her mind. Lea's breasts had already begun to develop and

Mother had cleverly disguised it when she made her dresses in order to protect her from being raped. Despite all the attempts of the military police to enforce the racial purity which was so noisily proclaimed, this was a particular weakness among rank-and-file German soldiers, who were probably like all other soldiers in the world. She had been afraid of this for her daughters ever since the awful moment when a German corporal with a mustache had boarded their train in Poland instead of a lieutenant. She couldn't be reassured, even by Father, who said, "For them, we're not even human beings, so what's there to be afraid of?" Katerina was the only one of her seven daughters she wasn't afraid about. Katerina Horovitzova remembered this now.

The first link in the chain was money—to pay for her family and then to pay the tailor and then the others.

The tailor squinted to dislodge a tear which nobody had noticed. He had not wept for a long time, because he'd got out of the habit. A new system of human relationships operated in the camp; a different scale of sensibilities and obligations had been established, different from the ones in the Five Books of Moses or in the writings of socialist scholars or even in sociology textbooks. With a certain complacency, he watched how the soldier was feasting his eyes and nerves upon the dusky temples of Katerina Horovitzova's creamy face, and as he watched he unconsciously granted Emerich Vogeltanz absolution for what had happened to him before he had left the workshop to come here and also absolution for her, for the fact that she had deserted her family in order to be able to leave the camp when they were unable to do so. Corporal Vogeltanz had come for him to the tailor shop. They made suits there for important members of the Gestapo, in addition to doing ordinary jobs on order for the German Army and fire departments in such distinguished old cities as Dresden, Munich, Stuttgart and even Berlin. At the door of the tailor shop, the corporal had impressed upon him the need for good behavior with these distinguished American gentlemen by striking a well-aimed blow against his forehead with the flat side of his bayonet. Following Mr. Brenske's orders, he went on to say that the job must be done by sundown, when Mr. Herman Cohen, his new ward and the other nineteen gentlemen would board the train again, which would take them west, away from what had once been Poland. First, the corporal asked the tailor how long he'd been in camp and when he answered that, altogether, he'd spent five years in this particular camp and the one before it, Emerich Vogeltanz informed him that in Germany, some people had already been in camps for eleven years, ever since the law was passed ordering protective custody for inferior races and for those who held incorrect or dangerous opinions. But he had questioned the tailor primarily to find out how much he knew about such things. He chuckled cunningly as he spoke, to show the tailor—if he was capable of understanding anything with that little artisan's brain of his—that he'd learned a lot from Mr. Friedrich Brenske and that this was all just a big joke. From the way he spoke, though, the tailor could not have many doubts. Still, he couldn't be sure of anything either. The impact of the cold steel blade against his forehead, done deliberately so that the bayonet just flashed past his eye, immediately set the proper tone with the tailor (in addition to the bruise) and his companions. It assured obedience and guaranteed that after he finished making the rich man's suit, he would be glad to be able to come back to the camp workshop and resume his usual routine while the twenty American gentlemen—with Katerina Horovitzova—would be facing the dangers which imperil any trip. Emerich Vogeltanz was both pleased and annoyed with himself as he watched the shabby tailor, wondering whether there was any point in devoting so much thought to such a wreck. He could hardly understand why he bothered. So he turned his attention to the dancer's legs and rubbed away the blob of spittle with the sole of his army boot.

The tailor had brought with him a suitcase full of sewing implements and fabric samples. He opened the lid and took out the swatches of material. They were beautiful Italian fabrics from the secret division's warehouse, brought straight from Via Vittorio Veneto in Rome. He handed the samples to Mr. Herman Cohen and Katerina Horovitzova so they could make their choice.

"Here are some samples, sir," he said. It sounded strangely affable.

Confronted with these beautiful fabrics, Corporal Emerich Vogeltanz realized suddenly that such lovely things are probably reserved for people who are richer and somehow more powerful than he. This conflicted with everything he had believed up to that moment. Are some people supposed to have everything and others nothing? He thought about the camp. This is probably the way it was outside the camp, and also here in the barnlike synagogue, where the powers endowed to the camp under the Nuremberg Laws do not exert any grip. The finest, most erudite and devoted minds in the Reich had worked out these Laws named after the ancient city. These twenty-one individuals were only a tiny minority, just a drop in the bucket in comparison to the camp. All right, who's supposed to have everything and who gets nothing, then? And for some reason, even though he knew a thing or two, Corporal Vogeltanz suddenly envied these twenty-one people. He felt that they were escaping from something. So were the others in the camp next door, but in a different way. How far do you suppose this beautiful hunk of girl will get? And Corporal Vogeltanz, whose father had been a sergeant in the Second Reich and whose grandfather had worn out plenty of army boots as a cannoneer, would have wagered that these distinguished civilians were going to slip away to freedom, even from Mr. Friedrich Brenske, who ought to have had them in the palm of his hand. He had been made responsible for this group because he had a lot of experience in handling people who couldn't be put away behind bars simply because somebody thought it would be a good idea. The corporal knew he shouldn't stick his nose in things which weren't any of his business, but he couldn't help it. After all, it had been Mr. Brenske who had summoned this dancer from Warsaw named Katerina Horovitzova to step out of the mob which was headed straight for the gas chambers. Corporal Vogeltanz felt an awful urge to sock somebody in the jaw. It didn't matter who it was, but he would particularly have enjoyed punching the rich American or else giving a couple of clouts to that pretty little Jew bitch who'd been hatched with such strange perfection from her mother's womb. But the secret division evidently had something up its sleeve which they weren't going to advertise. His mind kept going around in circles. Spitting on the floor wasn't enough. So out of the clear blue sky, Corporal Emerich Vogeltanz shoved the tailor sharply with his elbow so that he staggered awkwardly and felt the corporal's boot in his rear. He had just been bending toward the high window of the synagogue in order to show his fabric samples in the daylight. Without a word, he turned around immediately. His expression showed no reproach. He suspected why he had been punished.

"Excuse me, sir," he said. "I didn't know you were interested." This gave the soldier a plausible excuse and saved him the trouble of thinking up a reason for mistreating the tailor.

"Sorry," the tailor added and he moved aside so Corporal Vogeltanz could see the fabrics too. He had put everybody in a nervous, gloomy mood. They were reminded that the camp was right next door. This was all they knew. Nothing else.

"Yes, sir," the tailor added superfluously.

When he saw how Katerina Horovitzova was looking at him, Mr. Herman Cohen told himself he was a coward. He remembered what Oscar Lowenstein had said earlier, that they ought to look out for themselves, and he spoke quietly but emphatically: "We are under the protection of Mr. Friedrich Brenske here and the authorities under his command, I believe. He has personally assured me and, through me, the others in our group that our exchange for German war prisoners will be carried out without force of any kind and with full respect." When he spoke of his group, his voice dropped, as though he was excluding—regretfully— the tailor from his calculations. The tailor noticed the change of tone with resignation. "All of us realize," Mr. Cohen went on, "that these German prisoners of war will probably be very important people. It is quite possible, Corporal, that one of your generals will be among this group. Your superiors certainly realize this too. That is why I ask you not to use such methods in my presence anymore.

I hope you will be kind enough to avoid any more such incidents. Mr. Brenske himself has made it very clear that he has no time for brute force and we would like to believe that he means what he says. Anyway, I hope he'll be coming back any minute.''

Mr. Cohen wanted to add that he wasn't used to such behavior, but as he was making his wishes known to the corporal, he was made aware through every nerve in his body that the camp was right next door. The camp and everything that went with it: the ramp with its railroad coaches and tracks, the low sprawl of buildings with their stumpy chimneys. Even though he might not have known what made the greasy black smoke which kept pouring almost ceaselessly across the sky, the camp was there. So he kept silent. He felt an inexplicable anxiety. First there had been the spitting incident and now the way the corporal had shoved and kicked the tailor. It made no difference that all this had been directed against someone else, an absolute stranger, someone who was quite insignificant. It froze him to the ground, paralyzing him so he could hardly move; it was as though the inertia was spreading upward, all the way to his tongue and his lips. He couldn't do a thing. At first Mr. Brenske had explained that in a way, all this just reflected an abnormal situation, that usually there weren't so many soldiers in this part of the country. But suddenly Mr. Cohen was shocked by the disproportionate number of men in uniform who were guarding them. They ought to be able to expect absolute discipline from these men, just as Mr. Brenske did.

"That's all I have to say," he concluded wearily.

But the corporal had paid no attention to what he had been saying. He spat through his teeth, as though he had been eating sunflower seeds, which used to be the custom in this country when Herman Cohen had lived here as a child. He didn't even answer. Then, without any reason at all, Emerich Vogeltanz mumbled threateningly to the tailor as if he wanted to let off steam.

"You've got to go a whole lot farther than Jerusalem to learn what good behavior means. If it was anybody else but me, you'd already be dancing around with a lash against your backside."

He hardly knew how he found just the right words for the tailor, with his hunched shoulders, and for the other two, how he'd talked of "dancing" and hit upon his good old supercilious tone.

"One black-and-blue mark probably isn't enough to teach you a lesson. A bayonet's not big enough," he went on. "Once you're let out of the camp for a second . . ."

He sighed with almost genuine sincerity. But before Herman Cohen and Katerina Horovitzova had realized what had caused the bruise on the tailor's forehead, he continued, "You better get down to business now, and make sure the job's finished by sundown like they've told you so we don't detain these gentlemen."

The tailor apologized again. "Excuse me, sir," he said. Then, as though up to that moment he had been full of good will and a determination to get along amicably with everybody, Corporal Vogeltanz howled so loudly that his voice bounced back off the walls of the synagogue.

"Shut your trap, you goddamn wart hog! Who asked you anything, for you to keep on yakking the way you do? The only right you've got is to keep your mouth shut and watch your step. The camp's right next door. You heard what I said already. And if you think you're going to ask for help by passing some filthy scrap of paper you've got in your pocket, you'd better think it over before you make me twice as mad as I am already. We've got an apparatus next door that's tamed a lot of tougher little snots than you. And nobody smuggled out any pieces of paper from there. All you need to do is try and give me any more of your lip and my gun'll go off all by itself."

And then, as though he had never even raised his voice, he turned to Mr. Herman Cohen and Katerina Horovitzova and told them softly, "All right, you can talk to him again. He won't try anything anymore." It was as though he had been protecting them from the tailor. Everybody understood for whom his performance had been intended and why the corporal had spoken about "dancing" when he yelled at the tailor.

"Certainly, sir," the tailor said. He bowed his head in front of the soldier.

"Take the gentleman's measurements now. Otherwise you won't get done by sundown, needle-maestro."

"Yes, sir," replied the tailor with tremulous respect.

"First measure this gentleman and then the . . ." He didn't finish his sentence because he evidently didn't know whether to say "girl" or "young lady" or "Jewess." Anyway, they understood what was going on and Emerich knew they did. This gave him a queer, intoxicating thrill. "Do your duty, needle-maestro," he repeated, obviously fond of his new expression. "Orders are orders and sundown means sundown, so put your shoulder to the wheel. Well begun's half done."

Katerina Horovitzova shivered and told herself she must be careful. All the plans she had for her mother, father, grandfather and sisters had suddenly shriveled into a tiny lump of anxiety for her own self. She was ashamed that she was such a coward and she realized this, but Corporal Emerich Vogeltanz's shouts still echoed in the silence around her. She had been blaming herself ever since she got here that she'd behaved like a coward, but she made excuses for herself. She was more frightened now than she had ever been before. She wanted to save too many people, but she wasn't important enough to do it by herself. Maybe Mr. Herman Cohen and the other nineteen American gentlemen weren't important enough either. She hadn't even said good-bye to her father because all those people around him had been shoving forward since somebody had said the gas was "there." And then they suddenly started shoving in the other direction. Nobody knew where the beginning was and where was the end or what was supposed to happen to them now. All they knew was that the camp was huge and you couldn't see from one end of it to the other. Then she noticed that Mr. Herman Cohen's eyelids were trembling. He seemed to be blinking continually. Maybe she had always been more frightened of death than the other members of her family; maybe without knowing why, she wasn't as devout as they were. It was God's fault she'd had so many doubts about His omnipotent goodness when he allowed the Germans to make them suffer so, letting them be shoved around like a herd of mangy animals. Or perhaps it was because she had such a vivid imagination. She could visualize things with concrete intensity. After all, she had heard all along about the way they acted and what the camp was for.

She thought of Lea now, her pet, who had always looked up to her. There, her thoughts had swerved back to them again. Lea's childhood reminded her of a wormy apple.

They had grown up with the fragrance of wood shavings from their father's workshop. Sometimes Grandfather had reproached his daughter—their mother—for having given birth to someone so wild and lovely as little Lea, but Mother only smiled with silent pride. Her husband had fathered daughters in rapid succession, as though it were a punishment for having wanted a son so badly. Now, as Katerina looked through the fabric samples, she rummaged around in her brain for something which would cheer her up and drive away the fear she felt. She didn't have many memories to feed upon. Once, in Warsaw, before they'd had to board the train with the corporal with the mustache, a young man had come to their apartment on Low Street and suggested that Father and Grandfather consider the possibility of substituting an electric motor for their treadle-powered wood lathe. All they gave him was the same smile with which he later watched their Katerina dance. She looked as if she was snatching music out of the air whenever she danced. The Horovitz family was blessed with their girls, like a seven-branched candlestick, but they were constantly reminded that they must think about husbands for them in plenty of time. Grandfather and Father asked the young man pleasantly what would be the good of their legs if not to work the treadle of the lathe? They needn't wade through mud like soldiers, for instance, or traveling salesmen or messenger boys who worked for someone else. Wasn't it nice to be able to rest their fannies on the comfy rounded seats of the oaken chairs? Why pity their legs? Did legs have the right to an electric motor and idleness while hands and head went on in the same old way?

The young man was nice and he took a fancy to Katerina. She was twelve years old then and he'd invited her to dance during the intermissions at his union meetings, which had been noisy affairs where people kept shouting, "Wood-workers, unite!" She suddenly remembered the rhythm of the wood lathes where Grandfather and Father conjured up chess figures, insulation panels for electric switches and tool handles. In those days she used to dream of running away from home with the nice young man, all the way to France, which she knew about from reading Josephine Baker's story. She could imagine a cabaret floor, slick as ice on the Vistula in winter. The daydream had disappeared some-where and something else had come to take its place. That had been like a bridge and once you crossed it, you were suddenly grown up. This was how she felt right now. She was standing on the bridge and she must cross it, not just stand there, even though she might face fire and brimstone on the other side. She squinted as though a light had daz-zled her, leaving her blinded in the darkness.

"I hope you've heard those old sayings," said Emerich Vogeltanz to the tailor, "and that you've got them in your blood." And just to make sure, he repeated, "Well begun's half done."

The tailor took Mr. Herman Cohen's measurements. The tension which Corporal Vogeltanz had created did not ease even after the tailor produced his pencil and paper and tape measure from the suitcase. It all looked too shabby for the first-class work which was expected of him now. There wasn't enough ease in the air to fit on the head of a pin. And the tailor could have used some.

Mr. Herman Cohen pulled himself together again. By his behavior while he was being measured for his suit, he in-dicated to the tailor that he must watch his step and mind his manners from now on.

"All right, let's get on with this," he said, taking a deep breath as though he'd been running a race. He stretched out his arms just right, drew in his stomach and stood with his feet slightly apart, so the tailor could measure from the inside of his leg down to the heel to get the right length for his new trousers.

"All right, all right," the tailor wheezed. "Maybe there'll be enough material left over for cuffs and an extra collar. . . ."

The tailor was excessively cautious with Katerina Horovitzova. He barely touched her, clenching his pencil between his teeth like a horse's bit, then scribbling her measurements hastily on the paper. She had to take off her Warsaw coat and Corporal Emerich Vogeltanz imagined how it would be if she took off the rest of her clothes. The idea excited him, and he suddenly ran his tongue over his meaty, boyish lips. I bet you could have a lot of fun with this babe, he thought to himself as he stared at her mouth and her breasts. She chose the material for her new suit and coat quickly, pointing to the first swatch in the sample book. Thinking about her family, who were no more, and observing the behavior of Emerich Vogeltanz, the tailor coughed as though the invisible, reeking smoke from the adjacent camp were choking him. Too many black-haired girls have perished by now, he told himself; at least one of them ought to be able to survive. Maybe she had a special talent for discovering what was best for her, as she had done on the ramp. Beautiful people are always luckier, he thought, with inexplicable admiration and envy. Like the corporal. And considering what he knew about her family, her talent surpassed that of her six sisters. Ten people altogether.

"We'll probably have to make do with just one fitting,"

he said. Time was short and the gentlemen were in a hurry to continue their trip. "We'll have the things finished by sundown, as you said, with everybody else's help in the workshop."

Katerina Horovitzova didn't know what she ought to say. Herman Cohen spoke up. "At home, I usually have four, sometimes five fittings. Well, it can't be helped this time. We're in a hurry." But that didn't sound quite right, so he added, "Never mind; I'm sure the suit will be quite all right."

Again the tailor stared quizzically at Herman Cohen's shoulder pads, as though everything depended on them.

"All right, you, let's go," said Emerich Vogeltanz abruptly. "Quit stalling around now."

"All right, sir, I'm ready."

Mr. Friedrich Brenske appeared as soon as the corporal left with the tailor. He had evidently been waiting outside until they could be alone. Obviously he didn't count the silent guards.

So Katerina Horovitzova had no opportunity to take a deep breath and talk to Mr. Cohen about what lay so heavy on her heart, to ask him to help the other members of her family. She pressed her lips tight together, the grief and anger tasting bitter on the roof of her mouth. But the hope that perhaps, after all, she might escape tasted sweeter than she wished it did.

"When I make a promise, I keep it," said Mr. Brenske. "That makes me feel good and I hope you too. I'll try to go on being as obliging as I can. We realize who deserves what. Render unto Caesar and all that, serve those who deserve it. . . ."

The synagogue was built close to the ground, as though

the architect had been afraid of storms or the slightest external ostentation. But with the wing which had been built on, the humble house of worship temporarily provided enough space to shelter Mr. Brenske and his charges, even though it looked small and cramped. Considering what they had seen for themselves from the ramp, these were excellent accommodations. Mr. Schnurdreher said he had never been housed in a synagogue before and Mr. Taubenstock reminded him that, after all, it was only for a little while. And Mr. Rappaport-Lieben (who had insisted he wasn't going to take a step voluntarily when they had been put aboard the train in Italy, saying they might as well shoot him straightaway and get it over with) stood leaning against a wall, sound asleep on his feet. Of course he'd come along with the rest of them. He was dreaming that he was at the stockyards and all the dancers and singers from his Gondola nightclub were there too.

The guards had been waiting for them in the synagogue. No one in the whole group had ever seen such silent, impersonally stern characters as these guards.

"I'll be glad when we get out of this place," breathed Mr. Oscar Lowenstein. Then Mr. Vaksman asked why their passports had been taken away, but Mr. Brenske said this was just a detail, that they would get their passports back in plenty of time for their trip.

Mr. Klarfeld kept combing his hair and brushing off his clothes, while Mr. Rauchenberg peered sternly through his gold-rimmed spectacles as though he were trying to figure out whether they were really in danger or not. Under "Debits and Credits," Mr. Brenske kept an expense account in reichsmarks for their food and miscellaneous items like heating, lodging, transportation and "ransom fee," all payable in gold francs through a Swiss bank. Everything was carefully calculated, down to the last pfennig, and everyone was quite confident that they would receive a proper receipt for everything they were being charged. Right at the start, when they had been brought to the synagogue, Mr. Brenske reminded them that this was total warfare, being waged at great expense because of the immense consumption of steel and other materials. These charges might, to certain prejudiced minds, he said, be considered as somewhat of an abuse, even though he himself wouldn't think twice about it if the shoe were on the other foot. He was very willing to admit that war is a very expensive business and they shouldn't think that anybody was taking advantage of their situation by asking for payments. He was sure, of course, that German prisoners of war on the other side were not being treated incorrectly either and paying one's expenses is simply essential, since good relations depend on having one's business accounts in order. "Look here," he had said on the ramp when he had welcomed them, "this is going to cost quite a lot of money. But you've got the money and of course we know you have, so we expect you to be sensible and let us have it. You are in our hands and before we turn you over to your authorities, we expect to get something for our trouble. You are holding our prisoners of war on your side and there's a fantastic amount of money tied up in this. It's tremendously involved with morale and economics. You're too shrewd to need a lot of superfluous explanations. More people cost more money for our army and vice versa. When it's a war like this one, a matter of life and death, the German side—which I am representing—is fully within its rights."

Mr. Cohen had looked at him then almost with pity. This

was someone who could never in his wildest dreams imagine how many gold francs he and the rest of these distinguished American gentlemen could scrape together and boast about, if it weren't for what is known as business discretion, in bourgeois terminology.

He looked at the other gentlemen, who had understood, and at Mr. Brenske—concealing, along with the rest of them, a certain glee at the man's apparent ignorance. Or perhaps he simply underestimated them. The sum he mentioned was a trifle. Heat, lodging, even with the "ransom," came to less than one hundred thousand gold francs. It wasn't nearly as much as Mr. Brenske seemed to think it was. But nobody looked overjoyed; the realization swam deep beneath the surface of their behavior. Immediately they signed a transfer order for the money through a Swiss banking center.

Since Mr. Cohen and the others said nothing, Mr. Brenske continued. "If, God forbid, Germany should lose this war, it's a big question mark whether the Allies in the west or in the east would go to such trouble about us. Fortunately, this isn't likely to happen, though."

He paused in his speech for emphasis, adding that under such circumstances, all the little German boys and girls would probably have their heads cut off as Herod had done. Mr. Brenske indicated that this was an actual fact, not just legend, showing that he was well versed in history. The history of cruelty, anyway. Then he turned to the question of the exchange itself, reminding them that this was, as he put it, "an exchange of necessity, but an exchange it is, in fact." In arranging such an exchange, the side which Mr. Brenske was representing was entitled to receive a certain compensation. He was apparently primarily concerned that the twenty American gentlemen should realize this.

"It's possible, of course, that someday both western adversaries will join forces against an even more vicious enemy," Mr. Brenske added slyly, watching Mr. Cohen and the others. "In that case, to make it short and sweet, the money will stay in the same bank, so to speak, if not quite in the same family."

Mr. Brenske smiled frostily. The word "family" sounded ridiculous indeed. Anyway, he added apologetically, he was simply a civil servant for the Gestapo, not a diplomat, and that was why he was asking them to excuse the bluntness with which he may have inadvertently expressed himself in explaining all the basic positive and negative aspects of this case.

"But on the other hand," he pointed out, "the fact that you'll shortly be continuing on your way is certainly some compensation for all this inconvenience. Most people in the camp next door, if not everybody, would probably welcome such an opportunity. I'm almost positive of that."

Not very much was said after that about the bills being charged to the bank accounts of these twenty American gentlemen in the synagogue. But then all of a sudden Mr. Brenske came out with something that shocked Mr. Cohen and the others. In a dispatch from the secret division central information bureau in Berlin, Mr. Brenske had received a full report on Mr. Cohen's San Francisco bank account and on how much property the other gentlemen owned. The information was obviously based on their tax returns. Mr. Brenske spoke of "a nice little trough." That was how the others found out that Mr. Rappaport-Lieben's shares in the

Chicago stockyards amounted to more than "just a drop in the bucket" and that the nightclub he owned in another city was a real gold mine, as they say in the trade.

Mr. Rappaport-Lieben gulped and mentally relieved himself with two pungent phrases. The report had estimated that altogether, these twenty gentlemen had holdings worth between one hundred and one hundred fifty million gold francs, one-fifth in real estate, three-fifths in stocks and bonds, and the rest in cash. Mr. Brenske mentioned this in the same tone he had used at the beginning when Mr. Cohen still considered him simply as a courteous supplicant. Now everybody's cards were on the table.

"Let's sit down and make ourselves comfortable," Mr. Brenske suggested. "What do you say to that?"

Seated on the wooden synagogue bench, he crossed his legs casually, like an Englishman. He did not shout rudely like that young corporal, Emerich Vogeltanz, and that in itself was a relief.

Herman Cohen was almost relieved to hear what Mr. Brenske had been saying just before he'd suggested that they sit down. You had to give these Germans credit. They were smart and thorough.

But now Mr. Brenske told him he had come back primarily to find out whether he and Katerina Horovitzova were satisfied with the material they'd chosen for their new clothes. "I'm mainly concerned that you get rested up, so you feel as fit as possible. You've had a long trip and you've got another long trip ahead of you. You must break it up somehow. That's what I'm here for."

He added that he had just met the tailor and reminded him everything must be finished in fine style by sundown. And since, only God knows why, they had still been unable to locate Katerina Horovitzova's luggage, the tailor would bring along some other clothes when he came back to replace her own. The finest quality, of course, from the secret division's warehouse.

"I hope they'll be an adequate substitute," he told her. "We don't want you to be deprived in any way."

Mr. Brenske realized too that she was still a child. Or had been until just recently. He could tell by the lines around her mouth. There was a certain charm about this, but she was growing up. Clearly it was a matter of from yesterday to today, from today to tomorrow. Then Mr. Brenske asked Mr. Cohen to sign the receipts he had brought, which enumerated in neat, small letters and numerals the heating charges and estimated cost of cold food for their trip.

"You'll have to put up with rather modest fare at first," he said, "but it'll improve later on. Things must run in an orderly way. We want to make sure we are properly reimbursed in this exchange operation and we want everything to run as smoothly as possible. In other words, with a banker's tact. Yes, as I've already told you, brute force is quite alien to our nature. Great oaks from little acorns grow. Perhaps we're sometimes forced into using a bit of forcefulness, but it always goes against our grain and none of us ever enjoys it, of course. We aren't sadists. But we get what we want. You probably heard a lot of things about us before we came to Italy. It's all a lot of talk. If the Italians hadn't betrayed us and if Mussolini hadn't been kidnapped, we might never even have met. Now you'd better get ready for your trip. You're supposed to leave at sundown so your departure won't attract too much attention or perhaps cause envy over in the camp."

As Mr. Brenske said this, Herman Cohen almost absently

drew out his gold fountain pen and signed the receipts with two large, sprawling strokes. Again it was for ridiculously small sums. He might as well pay for it himself.

"Thank you," said Mr. Brenske with a gentle smile. "Nobody can see into another person's heart, so you probably don't even realize how glad I am when we can reach an understanding in a friendly spirit. We ought to be able to get along with each other. There are still a lot of things to be arranged but we'll cope with them together. By that I mean you in particular, though of course I'm not forgetting about the other gentlemen either. I'm always well aware that I'm dealing with an elite group of people. Perhaps I deserve some credit myself, but the main thing is you. All of you."

Then Mr. Brenske asked how the other gentlemen were feeling, as though he had forgotten that they were right there, scattered around in different parts of the synagogue building, each with his own guard. He said he was going to go around and have a word with each of them and in the doorway he instructed his lieutenant to stay with Mr. Cohen and Katerina Horovitzova in case they'd need anything, because the guards were forbidden to speak to them. And so Katerina Horovitzova lost her third and last chance to talk to Mr. Herman Cohen about her family. She gulped a few times and felt her lips grow dry. They were proud and desperate lips and her tongue was not enough to give them the moisture which a person needs when he wants to say something important. Mr. Brenske's eloquence hung in midair, along with the explanations he had given without mentioning the final outcome. The explanations and the outcome were intermingled.

Later, when Mr. Brenske came back, again almost at the

same time as the tailor, he said, "I've settled our financial matters with the other gentlemen by myself this time. From now on, you'll represent them and act in their name. Here I have their powers of attorney." He handed Mr. Cohen a sheaf of papers which needed only a transfer order to the Zurich bank and his signature.

"All I'm waiting for now is a telegram from Berlin," Mr. Brenske explained, "telling me whether I'll be able to go with you as far as the port and also from what port you'll be leaving and on what ship. Of course, on account of the unexpected difficulties this is creating for our authorities, you'll have to instruct your bank in Switzerland to pay the Reichsbank one million Swiss francs. That's going to cover all your expenses and with that our accounts will be settled."

Mr. Brenske peered at the synagogue's purple and orange satin draperies. What were they for? he wondered idly. Then, slowly and calmly, he turned his blue-green eyes back to Mr. Herman Cohen, who was gaping, his lips parted as though he were trying to form the sibilant *s* with his finely sculptured lips.

"A million gold francs?" In comparison to the carefully calculated sums for heat, light and housing, which were figured out to the last pfennig, this was exorbitant. "We didn't agree on that, sir. You yourself just said a while ago that the balance of the payment has already been taken care of."

Mr. Brenske smiled. He had a penetrating, hypnotic gaze and when he spoke to people, he always looked them straight in the eye.

"I'm sure these instructions will be sent out in time and my superiors hope so too so you'll really be able to leave by sundown. After all, I told you all this was quite unexpected. We certainly wouldn't want things to be held up, would we?"

There was a faint trace of military brusqueness, of something hard in what he'd said, but it dissolved in the cool, businesslike courtesy of his last words.

"It's all up to you. I'm being quite honest with you. I'm not hiding a thing. It wouldn't be in anybody's interests right now."

The tailor appeared with the two suits and the coat draped over his arm. Mr. Brenske's expression indicated that he did not want to say any more as long as the tailor was there.

He only added, "For twenty gentlemen who are as well fixed as you are, that amount of money surely isn't as exorbitant as it sounds when you hear it for the first time. Just think how much you'll still have left!" And then he remarked in a matter-of-fact tone, "Judging from the telegrams which have been exchanged so far—and which I haven't even mentioned so you wouldn't think I was trying to high-pressure you—it doesn't seem to us, after most carefully considering the content of these cables and the way they're formulated (personally, this struck me as quite deliberate), well, it didn't seem to us as though your officials are exactly burning with desire to exchange you for our prisoners of war. Not in this particular case, anyway. Of course, I have no way of knowing why this is. Maybe it's because you've all been away from home for a long time and because it's always easier to write off a person than anything else. But this whole exchange operation has encountered so many obstacles just in the stage of telegrams that the amount of money I mentioned, the sum we're asking for now—no matter if it does seem like quite a lot of money—is really hardly enough when you consider all the trouble this is going to give us and the cost. The main trouble was certainly caused by the fact that you're here and they are there. But that's not our fault. You gentlemen certainly deserve better than this, but ingratitude rules the world. This isn't the first case like this we've had. I myself arranged one such exchange of prisoners of war and again, I got the same impression even though that time the exchange was carried out in a spirit of harmony and to everybody's satisfaction. Well, I really must excuse myself now so things can be arranged by nightfall and so we can get this whole thing settled."

"Maybe those prisoners of war you're talking about are the kind which the side that captured them doesn't want to give up," said Mr. Cohen in a small voice.

"All right, but in your own way, you too are a big catch for us. There were two thousand of you and now there are twenty—twenty-one, that is. Of course, our high-ranking officers are not more than a handful among the many ordinary soldiers who are languishing away with homesickness. I'll put it to you straight: big fish for big fish, small fry for small fry. We hold you gentlemen in high esteem. You yourself have observed right from the start that we're not novices and that we know where money plays the main role. That's an exaggeration, of course." With his crooked smile, Mr. Brenske reminded Mr. Cohen of a blackmailer who holds the upper hand.

"That has been exactly our impression up to now," Mr.

Cohen said. "I'm sure this won't make a very good impression on my companions."

"Sorry," said Mr. Brenske briskly. "Now you know all there is to know."

"Let me think this over for a moment."

"That depends on what you mean by a moment."

"We're in your hands."

"Exactly," said Mr. Brenske. "And so you ought to appreciate it more than you do. I'd certainly have every right to feel offended after this little exchange of opinion we've had."

"But you're talking about one million francs!"

"All right, think it over."

Mr. Cohen and Katerina Horovitzova tried on the new clothes the tailor had brought; they were almost finished and few adjustments were needed. Mr. Cohen looked around and met the tailor's resigned and melancholy glance, then the startled, expectant brownish-green eyes of Katerina Horovitzova. She knew he had blundered somehow and that he'd probably go on making mistakes. It was no longer her family which was at stake now, all six sisters and her father and mother and grandfather. Now it was her own existence which was involved and suddenly, without another word, Mr. Herman Cohen signed a check for one million gold Swiss francs on behalf of himself and the other gentlemen. He signed his name with the golden pen and it looked only slightly less flamboyant than before. But he did not hand the check to Mr. Brenske. "I hope this will be all you're going to ask for," he said. "It's a lot of money. Even for big fish, as you put it, it represents a fortune, especially when you realize that you're fishing for something yourselves." He corrected himself hurriedly. "That is, you're asking for your own high-ranking officers in exchange for us."

Mr. Brenske raised his eyebrows quizzically and did not reply. Then, in order to make a good impression on Mr. Cohen and suppress any growing awareness that these men's value was going to diminish in proportion to the depletion of their money, Mr. Brenske asked the tailor where he had learned his trade, since everything had fit almost perfectly. He acted as though Mr. Cohen had simply forgotten to give him the check.

"I remember when I was a young man, I knew a fellow who worked in one of the best tailor shops in Warsaw," Mr. Cohen said. "But he got out in time. I think he went to Paris first and then to London."

"He probably had good advance information," said Mr. Brenske, smiling.

"Yes, he wanted to go to Vienna originally, but fortunately he thought twice about that," Mr. Cohen replied.

"Another tailor like that ended up in Gdansk," Mr. Brenske retorted and he was no longer smiling. His lips were thin and stern. But then he relaxed.

Mr. Cohen was still holding the check. He could feel how he was sweating and how his fingers were clamped onto it automatically.

"Let's not play games with each other. There's the camp right next door and I've still got a few vacancies left which I need to fill. I want this exchange of prisoners to really be an exchange. That's why I'm asking you to go along with me. You understand what I mean, I'm sure. After all, I can't hunt around now for twenty other people who'll be more obliging and more reasonable. I wouldn't even get the same satisfaction out of it either. We're counting on you. And we want to wind this up to everybody's satisfaction. I'd be awfully sorry if anyone made things hard for us."

The tailor slowly drew erect and stood in melancholy silence. The suit and coat for Katerina Horovitzova fit her perfectly.

Then slowly, complacently and with a very elegant gesture, Mr. Brenske took the check out of Herman Cohen's hand without even a glance at the signature and turned his admiring gaze on Katerina Horovitzova. At one time he had wanted to devote himself to the study of the occult and something of this interest still lingered.

"I've had some clothes brought over for you to replace your own things because we still haven't found your suitcase. You can try them on over there in the sacristy, if that's the right word for it. If you don't care for these things, just say the word. It'll be very easy to arrange things to everybody's satisfaction."

Katerina Horovitzova thanked him. There was perhaps an unintentional reserve in her tone, but she felt a shiver run through her when he spoke to her. Immediately she forced herself to be more friendly, but all she could manage was to nod her head.

"Do you suppose your workshop will be able to oblige us and finish these things by sundown as you promised?"

"Yes, sir. I'll be back by sundown."

The tailor was staring at Mr. Herman Cohen's shoulder pads again.

This time Mr. Cohen intercepted his look and deciphered it. Unexpectedly, he addressed the tailor. "You don't need to worry that I'll forget to see you get properly paid for this. I'll see to it that you get what you're entitled to and maybe even a bit more. I'm not just talking about your compensation, don't worry."

The tailor ignored his words as though they had not been uttered. Mr. Brenske frowned. It was hard to say whether it was because of the tailor's presence or because of Herman Cohen's delay in handing over the check. Now he stood silent for a while and thought things over.

Katerina Horovitzova went behind the curtain, where the Ten Commandments were kept in their cupboard. In the top compartment of the suitcase, she found a whole armful of exquisite lingerie. She made her choice rapidly, but she chose well. That was what she used to do at home too when her family asked her to choose her birthday presents. Maybe it really was because she'd been born on Sunday that she had good luck with whatever she touched. The fact that everything turned out well for her caused her almost as much anxiety as it did satisfaction. As the tide of hope rose and fell like a fever, she wondered how she could send a message to the camp. It took a while before she got an idea. In the bottom of the suitcase, underneath the thin cardboard partition for the underwear, she found the tailor's pencil and wrote a message in big letters so he couldn't help but notice.

"Mother, Father, everybody!" she wrote. "Before we leave here, I'll do everything I can so I can buy your freedom just like me. Cohen is a rich man and he doesn't mind spending money. I'm sure it will work out. Love and kisses, Yours, Katerina."

She covered the message with the rest of the underwear, feeling that what she'd written was not enough. She weighed every word against its opposite, hidden away in the depth of her heart. It seemed incredible that she would be allowed to leave when there was the camp, sprawled right beside them. Mr. Brenske had just reminded them of this himself. But why couldn't it happen to one single person, out of all those others? Why couldn't all these injustices be balanced by one single act of justice? Was she a coward because she wanted to get away herself? Or just the opposite? It wasn't easy to stay behind and it wasn't easy to leave either. There was something wrong with anything she tried to do. There was more evil in it all than goodness. There was no guilt and no innocence here, no crime on her part, just punishment. That was how it seemed to her. She closed the suitcase and set it beside her. She admitted to herself that to people around her, she probably really did seem prettier than other girls. But certainly worse than they were too. Why was it all so mixed up, so she couldn't tell what was good and what was bad and what term could be used for what she was doing? She didn't want to die and she had never harmed anyone, so nobody ought to want her to die. At home, all the seven sisters had been raised to respect life and to have compassion—and to behave with dignity. That included dignity toward oneself.

When she came out of what Mr. Friedrich Brenske had called the sacristy, she saw that he was being measured for the same kind of suit Mr. Herman Cohen had ordered. With the signed check for the Swiss bank tucked safely away in his breast pocket, he didn't seem to be in such a hurry anymore. He wasn't frowning either. So she wasn't surprised when he said he would wait there with them until the tailor came back with the clothes, and told his adjutant to bring any telegrams which came for him to the synagogue.

In place of the clothes she hadn't taken, he said, she would receive a fur coat as a personal gift from him.

"It just occurred to me that this would be only fair in your case, miss. Besides, if my memory doesn't fail me, some French writer once said that clothes enhance a woman's charms. It'll make me happy if it makes you happy too. War is war, but people are only human, after all. This binds us together, even though we are on different sides of the fence. But this shows you at least that I'm prepared to be lenient in some of the things we're forced to do. You must accept this as a gift from me. I consider it my duty to fulfill your slightest wish."

"I left the suitcase in there behind the curtain. . . ."

He refused her thanks and accepted her humble attitude with the frosty smile he reserved for official occasions. While they waited for the tailor to come back with their new clothes, Mr. Brenske passed the time with banal questions. He wondered how people were getting along on Mr. Cohen's side. He pledged them a safe trip to the port, "no matter which port it's going to be," he said. "And let's hope your planes won't shoot at you—or at me either."

"If word is sent off in time about who we are and where we're coming from, I'm sure there won't be any trouble," Mr. Cohen said.

"I'm not sure which route we'll be taking by rail and then which way we'll go by sea. Actually, I might as well tell you that these things aren't very certain these days." Mr. Brenske could feel that this made Herman Cohen feel a malicious glee like the time when he had first quoted those ridiculous sums of money for electricity and food and how much it was going to cost them in gold francs.

"The whole sea is thicker with mines these days than with fish," he said suddenly. "It's not just the sky that's dangerous. Besides, I'm not sure whether we oughtn't to ask our navy to clear the way for us first."

"I don't know what you mean. . . ."

"Of course, that would increase the cost," Mr. Brenske went on, as though he hadn't been interrupted. "Well, you'd have to talk that over with the other gentlemen and let us know in time."

This remark put an end to the anticipated objections before they had even been raised. He held out his cigarette case. Mr. Cohen thanked him, saying he didn't smoke. This was unheard of! But Mr. Brenske continued. "You people have always known what's best for you. You're quite right; smoking isn't good for anybody. Not always for me, even. They say people die because of their sins. Maybe so. But they don't have to. Not always, anyway."

He did not offer a cigarette to Katerina Horovitzova.

"Do you know by now whether we'll be going by land or sea?" asked Mr. Cohen.

"All I know right now is that I don't know a thing." Mr. Brenske chuckled. "But somebody else already said that, didn't they? We've got to wait till sundown. Sundown will take care of everything. And the sea is all around us."

Toward evening, the tailor returned with two large suitcases. He was again escorted by Corporal Emerich Vogeltanz.

"Well, that was really fast work," said Mr. Brenske.

"We were working at top speed and it's all finished, sir. . . ."

In the meantime, the corporal closed the door of the

synagogue so Mr. Brenske wouldn't feel a draft; he didn't suspect that the tailor had purposely left it open so he could tell Katerina Horovitzova that he hadn't been able to deliver the message she had written in the bottom of the suitcase. He feigned a cough and whispered, "That's a camp next door."

She racked her brain. What did he mean by telling her that? She was terrified. Just then Corporal Vogeltanz stepped back from the door and disregarding Mr. Brenske's presence, he cursed, complaining how cold it was on these damned Polish plains and what a nasty wind was blowing, which seemed to have no beginning and no end. "As though it was coming down out of the mountains someplace. But everybody knows there aren't any mountains for miles around."

"Take a look at yourself and see how nicely it fits," the tailor murmured, and in an even lower voice, he added, "There's nothing to change." He bowed his head and held out the new suit for Mr. Brenske to try on.

Mr. Brenske curtly refused to take off his trousers because he didn't want to in front of Herman Cohen and Katerina Horovitzova, but also because he didn't want to part with the small-caliber pistol he carried in his back pocket by order of the camp commandant, always cocked for immediate use. He never did anything that was against the rules and he probably didn't want to go into the sacristy for the same reason. So Herman Cohen's turn was next. A white basting thread dangled from the tailor's arm. Mr. Herman Cohen's trousers didn't need a single alteration. The jacket fit perfectly too.

"I'll leave you my old things," said Mr. Cohen. "Anyway, they won't do me any good anymore. That really is a nasty wind outside. I'll certainly be glad to get out of this place."

"Don't you like our wind?" asked Mr. Brenske benevolently. "Why, we're quite fond of it around here."

The tailor did not say what he was thinking just then—that this wind was howling now around the four points of the compass and across the whole face of the earth, blowing ashes across the land, which would soon resemble one huge graveyard. Pins were clutched between his clenched lips, their sharp points poking out like hypodermic needles. He turned slightly toward Katerina Horovitzova and passed his hand lightly across her shoulders.

"Not the wind . . . ashes . . . you'll probably be gone soon too." And then he coughed so neither Mr. Brenske nor the soldier nor even Mr. Herman Cohen understood what he had said. But Katerina Horovitzova, putting together all she had learned at home and all she'd seen here, finally understood something of what she had just heard.

His eyes reiterated something which had nothing to do with his work—that these ashes would be indestructible and immutable, they would not burn up into nothingness because they themselves were remnants of fire. They would not freeze, but simply mingle with the snow and ice, never drying under the sun's hot glare because there's nothing more to dry out of ashes. No one living would ever be able to escape them; these ashes would be contained in the milk that will be drunk by babies yet unborn and in the breasts their mothers offer them; the ashes will linger in the flowers which will grow out of them and in the pollen with which they will be fertilized by bees; they will be in the depths of the earth too, where rotted woodlands transform themselves into coal, and in the heights of heaven, where every human gaze, equipped with a telescope, encounters the invisible layers which envelop this wormy terrestrial apple of ours. These ashes will be contained in the breath and expression of every one of us and the next time anybody asks what the air he breathes is made of, he will have to think about these ashes; they will be contained in books which haven't yet been written and will be found in the remotest regions of the earth where no human foot has ever trod; no one will be able to get rid of them, for they will be the fond, nagging ashes of the dead who died in innocence.

The tailor's nostrils were full of these ashes by now and so were his eyes, and Katerina Horovitzova could see this but she didn't have the key which would have helped her to understand. She knew how to speak and how to be silent, using the same language as the tailor; after all, they both came from the same country; but she couldn't yet imagine what the tailor already knew for sure. He coughed continually now, and even though it had an ugly sound, she felt no revulsion toward him. At moments his eyes were wise and at other moments they looked quite mad. Later she was to see this same madness in the eyes of Rabbi Dajem from Lodz. She could not hear the tailor as he told himself that Mr. Brenske's lungs were full of ashes too and so were Mr. Herman Cohen's and Corporal Emerich Vogeltanz's and her breast too. In addition, she was inhaling the ashes of her six sisters, her mother and father and grandfather. She must not learn all this from words, but by reading it in his eyes, which always would be colored by these ashes. If the tailor had been a religious man, he would have said, "For ever and ever, amen," but he mistrusted things which were remote, because there was the camp, sprawled right next door. The camp was like a separate country, with its own frontiers, yet a world which had no boundaries at all. He knew about captured English, French, American and Canadian fliers who had gone to the gas chambers and nothing had happened, even though their papers had been in order. He hoped these rich men, waiting in the synagogue to leave, would bring the same price as a German general. Envy and good wishes had lost their original meaning.

He had made an extra pair of pants for Mr. Herman Cohen which he hadn't even ordered. Mr. Cohen lifted his feet as he tried them on so the cuffs would not touch the floor. A man who knew as little as Herman Cohen could discern only a vain sort of pride in the tailor's eyes, pride in his own handiwork and that of his fellow workmen and he did not recognize how helpless the tailor felt because he could not make Katerina Horovitzova understand the mute language of his eyes and of the ashes. And he could not manage to tell her more without using words.

The fur coat was beautiful. "I hope this makes up for her lost suitcase," Mr. Brenske said to Mr. Cohen. Then he turned to her. "Well, you're really outfitted like a queen," he went on. "I don't discriminate between you two, you see. After all, it shows a certain amount of authority in the way you're dressed now. And sundown is upon us. It's time to thank the tailor so he can get back to camp in time, according to the rules. Here rules go for everybody, including me."

The tailor turned to Katerina Horovitzova as though he were expecting to get a promised reward. Suddenly she understood the muteness of his lips, so she turned to Mr. Brenske.

"I'd like to say good-bye to my mother and father, if I may. Would I be allowed to kiss them good-bye?" She said it like a child. But she waited for his answer like a convicted prisoner who has reached the threshold of maturity.

The tailor stood there, hunched and staring at the floor.

Mr. Brenske smiled as though it were his own family she was talking about. "I understand how you feel, of course. But how can we do it if your loved ones are rather far away by now and since we must be on our way immediately so we don't run into any air raids? Now, how could we manage it?" He wrinkled his forehead and fingered his chin, pinching the pink and beardless skin like a wise man seeking a just solution to a difficult problem. In the meantime, Mr. Brenske's adjutant appeared, handed him a telegram and went away.

"We'll probably have to depend on what we might call the mail," Mr. Brenske added as he scanned the telegram. "You can write them a message on the bottom of the suitcase, for instance, under the lid of the underwear compartment, sending them your love and kisses and telling them you're sure things will work out just fine." He smiled gently, and looked compassionate. "It won't get lost."

Before anyone could say anything, he went on: "In a certain sense, the camp is a culmination. Every cause is at the same time an effect as well; each effect dissolves into itself. The human personality is not needlessly encumbered here with all sorts of extra frills and prejudices. If new arrivals are welcomed, there must also be good-byes. It's as though one, two, a thousand, even a million flames were merging together into one single bonfire. Thanks to magnificent organization, we can handle everything. Believe me, a lot of things which may seem almost impossible outside the camp are really looked at in the way I've just explained it to you. Why seek for something when it's already been found? And also, why punish when what we call punishment is really a reward? This camp covers everything, from christenings on up, and vice versa. Well, I've gotten off the subject, haven't I? I'll keep this in mind. Yes, yes . . ."

After a pause, he turned to the tailor with a scowl. Immediately the man snapped to attention; he had understood. "I'm sure you heard what we were talking about," said Mr. Brenske. "Tell them what nice clothes Miss Horovitzova has gotten and don't forget to mention the fur coat. Apologize for our haste, but you've heard what's involved. And don't try any tricks over at the camp." He turned to Mr. Cohen. "As I see from this telegram I've just received, the train for your group is ready and I've been allowed to escort you. It's a small transport. Our authorities have given their preliminary approval for Miss Horovitzova to be included in the exchange as Mr. Cohen's ward and of course he must assume all the legal responsibilities involved. Apparently an American passport with a visa for Miss Horovitzova is also on its way. We requested it through our consulate in Switzerland. Of course, not everything has been arranged entirely as yet, I must be honest with you, but this fact might also interest her family. We'll probably pick up her passport at one of the larger stations along the way, where it will be delivered by a special courier from the secret division so we won't be delayed. I won't have a moment's rest until I get a definite answer. On the other hand, I already know your port of embarkation and the name of the ship. It will be Hamburg and the ship is the *Deutschland*. A first-class boat, spacious decks, lovely cabins, good service and excellent food. The minesweepers which will escort us are ready too but they tell me here that these minesweepers are also asking for a certain fee. Here's the message."

Again Mr. Brenske smiled frostily, as though he had just remembered that Mr. Herman Cohen was there.

Scarcely without a second thought, Mr. Cohen took out his golden pen and signed the check on behalf of himself and the other gentlemen. This time his signature was small and cramped. Mentally he divided the whole sum by twenty. Even though it was a lot of money, it wasn't so excessive that their departure ought to be delayed because of it. He abandoned all his objections, including the reminder he had wanted to add that they were all intelligent people who had had a lot of business experience.

"Well," said Mr. Brenske to the tailor, "this is the beginning of the final solution. See if there's anything that needs to be altered on these clothes, then run along back where you belong."

"Yes, sir," replied the tailor and his head drooped as though it had fallen from a great height.

Quickly Mr. Herman Cohen held out his hand distractedly; he had in it a roll of dollar bills. The tailor slipped the money deftly into his own hand. He did not think anybody had seen it, neither Mr. Brenske nor Corporal Emerich Vogeltanz nor the four silent guards in the corners of the synagogue. But he wasn't sure.

"You needn't thank me. It was just our job," he said. "We did our best, but our resources are rather limited."

"I believe you," Mr. Cohen said disconcertedly. "Sure, I believe you. . . ."

He had been glad to hear what Mr. Brenske had said about the final solution and he took it to mean their financial affairs too.

Mr. Brenske had nothing more to say.

Katerina Horovitzova pressed the tailor's hand for a long moment, but she couldn't get a word past her lips. Either with his cap on or without it, he didn't look like a Judas who would have betrayed what she had written in the bottom of the suitcase. The meaning of Mr. Brenske's remarks was all too clear.

"I'll never forget you."

"I've got ashes in my eyes," said the tailor.

She pressed a long kiss against his lips. "For me, you are my grandfather and my father and my mother and my six sisters."

"Yes and no."

"Why do you say that?" she whispered.

"Let's get a move on," said Mr. Brenske. "It's time. . . ."

The tailor turned and left without another word, escorted by Corporal Emerich Vogeltanz. No one had to look at the dark bags under his eyes anymore or his gray, pathologically ashen face.

Mr. Brenske led Herman Cohen away to join the others; he wanted to say a few words to them before they left. For a moment, Katerina Horovitzova was left alone in the nave of the synagogue, dressed in her mink coat and looking like some famous European dancer. She felt as though she were coming down with a fever.

"I'm glad myself that you're getting away from here," Mr. Brenske said to Mr. Herman Cohen, just as the tailor had told Katerina Horovitzova. "I'm really in charge of all this from start to finish."

She could still feel the tailor's cold lips against her own.

TWO

S HORTLY AFTERWARD, twenty-one people stood out in the yard, hardly able to see beyond the end of their noses because it was already almost dark. The men in uniform who had been posted in close ranks inside and outside the synagogue and in the yard to guard each one of them moved in closer now. Together with the twenty-one shadowy figures, they seemed to form a sort of unit. The garden was drowned in darkness. Smooth-trunked walnut trees alternated symmetrically with pear and cherry trees whose branches drooped strangely close to the earth, and wiry gooseberry bushes concealed a tangle of young hazelnut saplings. The whole group looked as though it had been melted together into a single mass. Although no one felt much like talking, Mr. Brenske asked for silence because he wanted to speak to the whole group as he'd said he would and because he wanted to tell everybody in full detail what he had already told Mr. Cohen.

Smoke poured into the yard from the adjacent camp, darker than the twilight. It came in wave after wave, smelling strange. Katerina Horovitzova held her nose while Mr. Brenske was speaking. She couldn't get rid of the persistent impression that the smoke wasn't coming from the chimneys over the camp but out of Mr. Brenske's mouth. She kept denying to herself what she may have heard at home and what she had guessed from the tailor's words, as though such facts confounded even the understanding of those most closely concerned. What were they burning over there? What kind of rags and how many they must have! What was it that made her think of singed skin and burned fat? What could it be? She fought off the logical answer to her suspicions. She could no longer think rationally about the equation which she had drawn between cowardice and the desire to stay alive, but there were still a lot of questions which kept arising inside her mind. And none of them went away. The anxiety increased. Now there was Mr. Brenske who wanted to say a few words, and for many reasons what he had to say concerned her too. She tried to stand up straight, uncertain whether she should be happier if what he was going to say applied to her or if it didn't.

"Gentlemen—that is, Miss Horovitzova and gentlemen," Mr. Brenske began. "The moment has come for us to set out on our way toward the exchange which should crown our mutual relations and about which one of the best brains in international law has been negotiating, under Chapter Eight of the Legal Code, I believe it is—also about which it is difficult to speak without emotion because this is an exchange that deserves the blessing of both belligerent parties concerned and of such a noble, humanitarian organization as the one I have in mind: I mean the International Red Cross, which is really a splendid organization, an example of human charity in the right place and the embodiment of sacred principles applied in acts of compassion which embrace all mankind. It is up to us to see that this exchange of prisoners is carried out properly and to the very best of our ability. We know what this means, both for you and for our own soldiers who, maybe at this very moment, are gathered together prior to their departure just as you are here. It's not hard to imagine what they're longing for and to read their thoughts; very likely they're not much different from the thoughts you're thinking too right now. There was a time when prisoners from an enemy army were eaten and their heads stuck up on poles like trophies of war. There was a time when prisoners simply were not taken and when the sword, the knife and lethal bullets triumphed. Well, today prisoners of war on both sides of the battlefield and even those far in the rear need never lose hope that someday they will see their beloved homeland again, their dear ones, mother, father, grandfather, sisters and sometimes brothers too. They need not despair that they will never again be able to take up their plow or their hammer or go back to their drawing board. In other words, I am referring to all those things which together give meaning to our lives. The cloth of an army uniform binds people together regardless of where they come from; it creates a brotherhood in arms and this exchange is one of the many examples of tolerance in the midst of a sea of intolerance, an example of manliness and steadfast hope. The army's ABC's of ethics is quite clear on this, each letter in its proper place, just like over there in the camp, for instance, when it comes down to the question of life and death. You are the lucky ones who have been predestined by the lottery of social status not to have to stay here as prisoners, although here, too, I don't think you'll be going away without having gained a little bit more personal experience.

"In the port about six hundred miles from here, if you take into consideration the route we've chosen for safety's sake in order to confuse the enemy—excuse me, I mean your country's planes—in case they plan to attack our train, there in that port, as I was saying, a matter of between seven to ten hours from here, depending on how things go during the trip, a beautiful big luxury liner is waiting for you, the *Deutschland*. Aboard this ship, which has a registered displacement of fifteen thousand tons gross, great events have happened, events of which history books will write someday. From its deck, for instance, our own Adolf Hitler"— when he said this, the soldiers snapped to attention and even a few among the other twenty-one unconsciously drew erect—"watched the last great prewar naval maneuvers in the Baltic Sea. By now, the gallant deeds of our navy, our magnificent fleet of submarines, our wonderful torpedo boats and glorious minesweepers, our invincible PT boats and unsinkable battleships, are all in their way incarnated in the very name of this great vessel, which is both passenger liner and battleship, the *Deutschland*, which has been assigned to us, a vessel forged and constructed of the purest metals and welded together with blood and fire, even though everybody knows that today, in time of war, every last tub, if I may put it that way, is needed to defend our shores. But I don't mean to stray too far from the subject. We're defending ourselves valiantly, but while the god of war thunders, we do not close our eyes to those who are not at war just now. To get you back to your people and our captured soldiers back home again is the whole purpose of this voyage. This is the strict and honest formula, red-blooded and humane, part and parcel of our ABC's of ethics, a direct reaction to their spirit and letter and to the concepts I've already mentioned.

"Now, without a lot of long and unnecessary talk, let's get down to business. You hold passports of a power which is our enemy—that is, at the present time, at least. But in your cases, this power has agreed to an exchange—man for man, piece for piece, you might say. We were even permitted to include in your group a woman who was chosen by one of you, that is, by your intermediary and spokesman, Mr. Herman Cohen, whom I wish to thank on this occasion for his good services up to now. In view of the fact that those others are for the most part officers of no great means, regardless of what high rank they may hold and what valor they have shown and will certainly continue to display—and I might add here that they surely haven't either asked for or received the special treatment you have been given—so, in this case, all expenses involved in this operation will be met by you. The German Reich accepts this contribution with thanks and we will not forget it. Already now your privileged position has been recognized. As the head of your group—my name, as many of you already know, is Friedrich Brenske, and I am a commissioned army officer—as, I repeat, your leader who has been assigned the responsibility and, I'm pleased to emphasize again, been given the permission to accompany you, I shall be going with you to the point of rendezvous, which will be communicated to us by telegraph once we are aboard the *Deutschland* and then, after the voyage is over, we will drop anchor and dock so you can walk down the gangplank. Right after that, our soldiers will come on board.

"I hope that you will not forget either that our Reich has undertaken this operation—keeping in mind, of course, our own soldiers over there on your side—at a particularly critical time. The innumerable tentacles of war reach out on every side and these must be destroyed or put to use; we are mobilizing all our available resources against practically the entire world. Despite some almost superhuman acts of heroism, we're only human, all of us. It may be that things have gotten a bit out of hand at times, even though it was only briefly, and maybe there were moments—which I very much regret—when you felt intimidated by these armed guards. You had endured a long trip from that sunny land which betrayed us, you hadn't much to eat or drink and you were probably even denied the comfort of a good night's sleep. The noise and lack of fresh air have taken their toll and maybe you were a little bit oversensitive, too, to the fact that this whole operation and transport were undertaken hastily and perhaps a bit nervously. Indeed, something of the anger we feel at every act of betrayal has probably rubbed off on you indirectly. A personal friend of our Führer was taken prisoner, your troops had landed on the territory of our Axis ally, your planes had bombed us, burned bridges and highways ahead of us and behind us, and they have continued their piracy. I'm sorry. I can assure you that I regret this whole thing most sincerely and it is our Reich which speaks to you now through my lips. Also, don't pay any attention to what you may have heard from irresponsible individuals on the station ramp; we realize very well that these were disturbing rumors. We have taken note of these remarks and we can disprove them, regardless of whether these are charges, as we've been told, of arson, pillage and robbery, persecution or murder. These are—

and you can trust me—simply malicious and evil words. If any of these things have upset you at any time during your stay with us, I would like to apologize on this occasion for our soldiers and to express the hope that you will accept my sincere apologies. All's well—and I want to state this here and now—all's well that ends well. I'd even go so far as to say that everything will come out right in the end. Someday people will forget about the towns which have been destroyed and about all the villages which have been burned down, as new and better towns and villages are built. New babies will be born to take the place of those who've died and they'll grow up into new people. They'll be more enlightened, better educated and maybe even more resistant.

"If you will accept our apologies in part, at least, we'll consider this as a friendly handclasp between you and us, and once you've reached your final destination we're going to ask one more thing of you. Maybe I'm getting a bit ahead of myself, but I want to get everything off my chest at once. When you reach your final destination, we hope you'll find a good word to say about our country. This war has been forced upon us. We didn't have enough room and even today we're overpopulated. Every German mother, when she gives birth, must ask herself whether she hasn't made a mistake by bringing into the world a new young hopeful for the Reich. And this is just one of the many bitter questions they must ask themselves. These children will grow up and they'll want to plow and sow and there will be new mouths waiting to eat the fruits of their harvests. That is why, instead of scythes and factory whistles, our fine young soldiers have taken up arms which have been forged out of plowshares and hammers and why, from the river Rhine to the Danube or the Vltava, they hear the roar of cannons instead of our good old German folk songs. They are fighting and dying so they may go on living. We don't always act the way your newspapers and radio say we do and like our enemies number one, two, three and right on down the line say we do, like all our enemies say we do, right down to the very last one, closing their eyes to the truth. By that I don't mean the great mass of the people. There isn't a grain of truth in the accusation that just a few weeks after we took power we were already operating forty-three other camps just like this one. You can't simply blame us unilaterally for the cities which have been destroyed, the hundreds of thousands of villages which have been burned down and the millions of widows and orphans, for the endless streams of refugees on Europe's highways. Even today there aren't many camps like this one—not as big as this, anyway—and there won't be any, once we get rid of those who oppose us.

"I am appealing to each and every one of you so that once you reach the site of the final solution and stand beyond this world of ours, you will combat those fallacious slanders which sometimes still put us in such an unfavorable light. This is awfully important for us. Maybe the slanders about our Reich and the aims we're pursuing aren't as dangerous for us as it might seem from what I was saying at first, but they're irksome, like fleas for a purebred dog, like a leech on an open wound, or as if a poisonous insect had laid an egg in your eye or inside your ear. Every state lives according to its own definition of right and wrong. The more consistent its aims, the stronger the country. From your standpoint, our theory may seem to be prejudiced against your race, but in some instances your race has really shown itself to be hostile toward what we're trying to do. Also, it's

68

not out of the question that after a while, some of our principles may be modified in some respects. After all, gentlemen, your case itself shows that cooperation can exist in this area, regardless of boundaries and other differences. We won't rule out further cooperation of this kind, either. Today it's you and your money which are important for both sides. Tomorrow it may be your trucks and gasoline and airplanes, your guns and gas, and our soldiers and our people which will be important to both sides. You in your country realize what insects are good for and we know the kind of gas to use to get rid of insects in the metaphorical and absolutely literal sense of the word. Each one of you will witness the most magnificent harmony among these elements in human history. That's why I want you all to work toward mutual understanding. Disseminate the truth wherever you go. There can never be enough truth. I'm asking you to do this as your friend and as someone who is responsible for you and who, for a while, has been made responsible for your fate just as though you were soldiers. I have been ordered to look after you as if you were our own people or someone who is important to us. I tell you this again as an officer who places the highest value on what we call so inadequately military honor.

"Well, gentlemen—and Miss Horovitzova—the International Red Cross has made itself responsible for your safety and its governing body is already working with all its might toward this end, and under its protection we will shortly be starting on our way. We've just been waiting for it to get dark enough and now I think it has. Thank you for the understanding you've shown so far. There's no time now to go into things in detail, but I would like once again to apologize for any of the shortcomings or lapses of discipline which may have occurred. You've got to try to understand these soldiers. We have treated you like prisoners of war. You've been isolated from each other and outside the camp territory. That's what the law stipulates and my orders are the same. A prisoner is an item which is not included in the definition of either a soldier or a civilian, but in every respect, a prisoner, military or civilian, is closer to the first category. Now, in conclusion, I repeat: the hour of twilight has arrived, which was the time when we were supposed to leave. Soon we'll board the train and then, after our trip is over and we reach the port of embarkation, you will board your ship. Once on board, you will receive further instructions for the rest of your voyage. Our men whom you see here will accompany you to the compartments which have been assigned to you. There will be one person to each compartment and there will be two guards inside each compartment and one outside in the corridor. We are obliged to provide proper surveillance during the whole duration of your trip, which shows how concerned the Reich is with your safety. During the trip, the two coaches will be connected by an open walkway. Circumstances make all this necessary. I would like first of all to draw your attention to one more thing. Window shades will be drawn during the whole trip in order not to betray our position to the enemy. We are also doing this, to be quite honest with you, because we do not want to irresponsibly give away the location of installations of military importance along the route we'll take to anyone not bound by our oath of allegiance. However, you'll have a blue control light on inside each compartment during the whole trip. You will be transferred to the ship through a carefully assigned corridor. This is essential for reasons of military security. But otherwise, everything will be as free and relaxed as possible. On the way, you will be able to eat and drink more than enough for such a short time. You'll have the same food and drink as your guards. We've also prepared a little refreshment for you in farewell. Of course, we can't serve you hot meals. If anyone suffers from seasickness, we've even thought of this and you'll be able to get special treatment. And finally you will arrive, unharmed and unshaken, at your destination. I wish us all a pleasant trip. I'm sure that later on you'll look back on this evening, on this whole trip, and that you'll even remember me, without the least hard feelings."

Mr. Brenske coughed. The whole speech had been delivered in a cultivated tone; the phrases had been well chosen.

"Well, then, gentlemen, that's all I wanted to say right now. Does anyone have any questions concerning the trip itself or about any of my remarks, or is there something I may not have explained in sufficient detail?"

"When will we finally get our passports back?" Mr. Walter Taubenstock asked Mr. Herman Cohen in English.

Herman Cohen translated it and Mr. Brenske replied without a moment's hesitation. "Just as soon as your name is called from our list and you board the train."

"Thank you," replied Mr. Walter Taubenstock in rusty German.

"How come we're being guarded like a whole enemy army?" asked Mr. Freddy Klarfeld.

Mr. Oscar Lowenstein repeated the request he'd made several times before. He wanted to talk to a representative of the International Red Cross. Apparently he knew something about such procedures, since one of his relatives was on the board of governors, but again Mr. Brenske reminded them that in their case, which was exceptional and conditioned by the needs of war, he himself was their sole intermediary, so he must ask Mr. Lowenstein and the other gentlemen for their continued confidence in this delicate matter.

"I'm sure that in the end, you'll have no fault to find. All I can do is to repeat all the assurances I've given you."

At that moment he sounded almost supplicating. He had smiled when he said "I'm sure" and after that his face looked stern.

One of the gentlemen remarked that Mr. Klarfeld was splitting hairs unnecessarily. They kept telling him that during the rest of the trip. Someone else asked about a receipt for the money which they had paid. A few other questions were ignored as being too petty.

Herman Cohen had been momentarily embarrassed by Mr. Klarfeld's question, which somehow remained hanging in midair, but finally transmitted it to Mr. Brenske.

Mr. Brenske smiled frostily as he had done before. "This is war, gentlemen, to put it bluntly, and in wartime, rules are a lot stricter," he said. "Even in your country, I couldn't parade around freely in a prisoner-of-war camp without any control and without being told where I could go and where I couldn't. What if someone got it into his head to do something dangerous? Please try to understand my position. This question takes in a lot of subsidiary questions. It isn't easy to get from here to the other end of this camp, not to mention arranging a trip all the way across this huge hinterland, which is one of the pillars on which a whole front is based. That means there are millions of men whose rear we must protect. Do I make myself clear?"

Nobody knew exactly what he meant by that, but that was all he had to say to Mr. Klarfeld's question.

"What were they saying about gas there on the ramp?" Mr. Rappaport-Lieben asked suddenly, but the other gentlemen immediately started talking to him in rapid English and Yiddish, even though he'd asked the question in Polish. In this way, the whole question was drowned out by their words and Mr. Brenske didn't try to find out what he had said, although he had obviously understood.

"Gentlemen—and Miss Horovitzova," he said almost apologetically, "believe me, from the bottom of my heart, I'd like to talk with each and every one of you individually and at great length. Actually, there's not a single one of our plans about which you haven't been personally informed, at least in a general way. But now you see that dusk has fallen on heaven and earth and we must hurry. We must finish what we've started. We can do it with or without a lot of philosophizing, by debating or not. The end result is the same, I promise you that. We're all in a hurry to wind up the problems connected with your exchange. We—and you too—are concerned right now with getting this over with, as we say it plainly in the army. Thank you for your understanding. And now if you'll please follow me . . ."

"Where are we going in this darkness?" murmured the incorrigible Mr. Freddy Klarfeld.

"Take my arm," Mr. Brenske replied. And he guided Mr. Klarfeld until he felt secure enough to walk by himself.

Mr. Rappaport-Lieben grumbled that there might be something to the question he'd just asked.

Mr. Friedrich Brenske cleared his throat almost absently. After they had groped blindly for a while through the darkness, Mr. Rappaport-Lieben's tactlessness was forgotten. Everybody had enough to do to watch out for himself.

When Mr. Schnurdreher stumbled and almost fell, Mr.

73

Brenske helped him up and Mr. Rappaport-Lieben lowered his large, almond-shaped eyes in a mixture of shame and rebelliousness. He had no more to say about Mr. Klarfeld's and Oscar Lowenstein's complaints, either.

By itself, the group fell into line. Each of them had a guard at his left and one at his right. The guards smelled of mothballs and ersatz cloth and a strange kind of boot grease; it was a rather pleasant smell and it burrowed itself deep in their nerve endings and in their memories. Mr. Brenske was accompanied by his tall adjutant, who showed the way with a blue-shrouded pocket flashlight. They emerged from the garden and came to the path. Everybody noticed the low red flames above the chimneys and that same strange odor. Right behind Mr. Brenske came Herman Cohen and after him, Katerina Horovitzova. The others were silent, except for Mr. Rappaport-Lieben, who brought up the rear. He was the only one who kept on mumbling, until his guard had to prod him with his gun butt, which went unnoticed in the darkness.

"We don't do things by brute force. We prefer the friendly way," Mr. Brenske said just then, smiling into the shadows. "It's in your interests and ours too. That way, we both show ourselves in the best possible light. On we go, gentlemen, on we go." He was like a wheedling father or uncle or else the commander of a veterans' corps.

They were evidently near the ramp where they had been that same morning. Several long freight trains were pulled up on a siding where tall concrete pillars reared up into the dusk. Neatly woven high-tension wire with shiny white porcelain insulators was stretched across twenty-five-meter intervals between these pillars. The wires were as taut as the strings on a musical instrument, but they made no music. Or at least they didn't seem to. Flames still belched and roared from the same chimneys of those low buildings which looked like factories or crematories, but it hardly seemed as though there could be so many crematories so close together. The flames noisily illuminated the smoke which still hung over them. It was black smoke, as though even the redness of the flames could not ignite them or give them color. They could have been brick ovens or tannery sheds or incinerators of some sort. Under the ceiling of the sky, the smoke mingled with the deepening twilight so that it might have given some people the impression that there was nothing but smoke for miles around. But in the background, trains and locomotives shuttled back and forth, then moved away, sparks seething, then suddenly extinguishing themselves. Out of the darkness came a strange roaring noise. Something was happening all around them but they couldn't figure out what it was.

"What's that over there?" asked Mr. Schnurdreher.

"Go and see," replied Mr. Rappaport-Lieben in a strangely irritable voice.

But there was no time for that, even if they would have been allowed to and if Mr. Schnurdreher had really wanted to.

Mr. Brenske stopped on the ramp next to one of the trains. This made the others think this was their train and they stumbled to an abrupt halt like a herd of sheep or a mob of army recruits.

"I'll read off your names one after another and then you may get on the train," said Mr. Brenske. "Slowly, carefully. Don't rush. Behave in a really disciplined way. For your own good, we don't want any accidents at the very last minute. Get ready now. You can't imagine how sorry I'd be if any of you hurt himself. A sprained ankle or, God forbid, a broken leg or arm would throw off my whole calculations, timewise and administratively. So be very careful. Are you ready? There's plenty of room for everybody; you don't need to worry. All right, then, let's go.''

The words fell into the darkness and gently soaked into the silence which came before and after that loud roar which no one had got accustomed to. Now the blue flashlight in the adjutant's hand was turned on a typewritten list of names. The adjutant was a husky young man, straight and tall as a candle. He was doing his duty.

Herman Cohen, standing next to Mr. Brenske, saw that Katerina Horovitzova's name was first on the list and his was last, as though the two of them stood apart from the other nineteen. He was sorry they wouldn't be traveling in the same compartment, but no one was allowed any companion besides his guards. With a shabby sense of relief, Mr. Cohen bid farewell to the camp and suddenly he remembered the tailor who was for him its very incarnation.

Wearing his new suit, he suddenly felt better than he had for a long, long time, but then he was full of self-reproach. Well, so we're really leaving after all, he said to himself, no matter how strange and suspicious everything had seemed to some of the gentlemen after what they had heard and what they had been able to figure out for themselves. He thought about what Mr. Schnurdreher and Freddy Klarfeld and Mr. Rappaport-Lieben had said and he put it quickly out of his mind. He wished he were already in some place of safety from which they could all look back at this and laugh, but he dared not do it ahead of time. It didn't seem quite suitable in such a place as this.

76

Mr. Friedrich Brenske ran his tongue over his lips as he'd done when he began his long speech. "All right, now . . . Katerina Horovitzova, please."

Then the others' turns came: "Adler Hans, Arnstein Vladimir, Bettelheim Jan, Ekstein Oldrich, Gerstl Stepan, Ginsburg Johann, Klarfeld Freddy, Landau Samuel, Rappaport-Lieben Miroslav, Lowenstein Oscar, Rauchenberg Otto, Raven Sol, Rubin Leo, Schnurdreher Friedrich, Siretzsky Milan, Taubenstock Walter, Vaksman Jiri, Varecky Josef, Zweig Benedict and Cohen Herman."

Mail coaches with barred windows and a single door were about three cars behind the locomotive; only somebody with better eyes than Mr. Rauchenberg—Mr. Zweig, for instance—would have been able to see that. The next two coaches still bore the insignia of the old Wagons Lits. They were comfortable-looking coaches with red roofs and nice big windows, even though they offered no view because all were tightly curtained. The guards obviously already knew who belonged where; they got busy as soon as Mr. Brenske started reading off the names and surnames, so the boarding went without a hitch, except for Mr. Taubenstock, who asked for his passport before Mr. Brenske got around to that.

"I don't know why all this stalling around," he objected. "I'm paying, fair and square, and I want my passport back. It's my good money."

He was assured he'd get everything that was coming to him.

"I'm fed up with all this fooling around," he insisted. "This isn't the way to do business."

"Now, don't get upset," said Mr. Brenske. "There are just a few last-minute things to do before we leave. If you

77

weren't here, not even your passport would do you much good." Mr. Brenske smiled complacently and was the last to board the train. "Well, here we are at last, all together."

A seat reservation card was hung in the doorway of each compartment in both coaches, bearing names and passport numbers, and there on the striped plush seats lay the passports. Two of the bars on the window grilles served as flagpoles and there, like sisters, glistened two handsome little flags, the swastika of the German Reich and The Star-Spangled Banner of the United States of America.

"There you are, gentlemen, proof that promises must be kept and trust in turn deserves trust. Well, maybe we Germans always have been a bit more generous and broad-minded than other people. Except our tolerance is mingled with efficiency and that's what makes us different, probably better in some ways, even though we might seem kind of stodgy at first glance. I said you'd get your passports back and now you have. A German officer is as good as his word."

Everybody's passport lay on the seat inside the door, looking as casual as if this were a college excursion chaperoned by members of the faculty.

Mr. Brenske's words suddenly fell on fertile soil, even though he'd said it all before. No one spoke a word.

Mr. Taubenstock couldn't restrain himself and grabbed his passport with both hands like a child who has been deprived of a favorite toy for a long time. Two guards sat, facing each other, with each passenger in his private compartment, while still another stood outside in front of the door. With their passports in their hands and seated in these comfortable compartments, they all suddenly felt quite festive and even the presence of the guards seemed quite natural. Everything had happened exactly as it had been planned, down to the last detail. Two packages of cookies lay at the far edge of each seat.

"I told you all's well that ends well, didn't I?" remarked Mr. Brenske. "Our trip together will be that much more pleasant."

By now everyone was seated and Mr. Brenske made the rounds to ascertain that everyone was as comfortable as possible. Then he reported back to Mr. Herman Cohen.

"Well, everybody's nicely settled and we can get under way. All that's left to do is sign for the designated amount of money to cover fuel for the ship and wages for its crew and their equipment, which I'm afraid we'd overlooked. I'm sorry everything couldn't be submitted at once in a single bill, but I didn't know about this any sooner myself. Then, too, even though there was some mention of this before, we forgot to charge you for the job of clearing the way for the ship. Altogether, it comes to one hundred thousand gold francs multiplied by two—not as much as I'd originally expected. I'd like to be able to wire ahead that these payments have been arranged before we leave so our trip won't be interrupted by any unpleasant misunderstandings. I like a clean slate and to have things shipshape. You've probably already noticed that yourself."

He smiled almost apologetically.

"All right, if this is the last one hundred thousand francs multiplied by two," said Herman Cohen, his joy at their imminent departure slightly tarnished now.

But it really wasn't so much money, considering it meant that they were finally on their way to freedom. Of course, this was all blackmail. That was clear by now. But here they were in the train, they'd got back their passports and somewhere up ahead was their port of embarkation. And there beside the train was the camp, and Mr. Rappaport-Lieben's question—"What were they saying about gas there on the ramp?"—didn't come out of thin air. The most valuable thing a person has, Herman Cohen thought to himself, is a sound head on his shoulders and you can lose that only once. But you can keep on earning money over and over again. For some strange reason, he thought of sunken treasure and all the galleons which had gone down, taking along their crews and gold, down to the bottom of the sea. How was it that when anybody talked about lost treasure, it was only the gold they spoke of and not the people? How many ships had sunk to the bottom in these gloomy regions? And so he signed his name with minuscule fancy flourishes, finishing—or so he thought—the final stages for their departure, in the name of the nineteen other gentlemen and one young lady. Mr. Brenske bowed like a bank clerk and left the compartment; from the corridor, he turned to ask Mr. Cohen to "look after your people from the administrative aspect," as he put it smilingly, and handed him several lists.

"All right, everything's ready to go. Are you? So are we," he said.

Night had almost fallen, the dusk had thickened, and Herman Cohen nodded.

"We're all set," he said. It had almost a military ring to it.

Mr. Brenske nodded to the guard who was standing in the doorway and he in turn passed on the order to the engineer. Slowly the train huffed out of the station.

One by one, the doors latched shut. Money buys everything, almost everybody was thinking with a certain complacency, with the possible exception of Mr. Rappaport-Lieben and maybe even he thought so too. It had cost a lot of money, but they were on their way at last. As the last door closed, Mr. Klarfeld caught a glimpse of the station semaphore and contentedly savored its glow, which was muted because of the blackout. The red flames roared over the chimneys into the night and finally even they disappeared as the doors in the railroad coaches were all slammed shut.

It would be hard to describe the emotions of Herman Cohen and the other nineteen men and Katerina Horovitzova as the wheels rang over the steel bolts which riveted the rails together. Now for the first time, with the sound of movement, it all seemed credible and they were profoundly grateful for the very fact that they were moving, quite apart from the direction in which they were headed and their final destination. A suspicious kind of hopefulness prevailed among their varied emotions, along with an appreciation for Mr. Friedrich Brenske. He had kept his word, regardless of how expensive it had been for everyone and no matter how questionable his behavior had been and the difficult circumstances in this country. Railroad coaches, which were in short supply even for military purposes, had been made available for them, and guards who might have been sent to the front were wasting their time and fighting power here. There were too many contradictory impressions crowding in on all the gentlemen with American passports. And then there was always the constant and insistent proximity of that evil camp and everything connected with it, the ugly, secretive buildings with their squat chimneys, the very enormity of the camp, which gave the impression of immense efficiency even though Mr. Brenske had spoken of complications which might arise and once—as they all remembered—about the possibility of contagious disease. Everything had been well organized and now here were their passports in their hands or in their pockets. This carried a lot of weight and so did everything else, even if they had been leaving the place stark naked. Suddenly they stopped regretting how much it had cost them. It was as though they'd forgotten all about the money they had had and didn't anymore, which usually happens only to people who are blessed with the gift of improvidence, even though instinctively they strongly disapproved of this reaction. But no matter what happened during the rest of the trip, nothing could be as bad as the camp.

The wheels picked up speed, clicking faster and faster against the rails. Now the train was no longer getting started; it was speeding through the night, whizzing along through winds which probably were purer now than they had been back there at the camp, streaking through the darkness of the night which no one saw because of the blackout curtains and the dim blue lights inside. Considering their age, the coaches were very well kept; the compartments were cozy with their plush and leather upholstery which the guards seemed to appreciate. It probably wasn't right to feel sorry for the guards who had to stand outside in the corridor, leaning against the door. Mr. Herman Cohen and some of the other gentlemen would probably have been pleased to invite them to come in and take a seat in their compartment without any ulterior motives, assuring them that they needn't be afraid they'd stage a mutiny. Mr. Rappaport-Lieben was probably the only one who didn't feel quite the same way, and neither did Katerina Horovitzova. Regardless of her gladness, suspicion gnawed away at her, along with feelings of self-reproach because of those she had left behind in the camp without even saying good-bye. It was true that she herself had not been strong enough to change anything in this carefully planned, efficient organization where one individual didn't mean a thing. She remembered the tailor, who had represented for her all the members of her family, and then her joy evaporated. But it came back again as the train sped on. She didn't notice how the two guards were looking at her. They glanced knowingly at the fur coat on the hanger inside the door. For her, too, the iron music of the rails and wheels was sweet to hear and their melody left almost too much room for her vivid imagination. She felt like a bird huddling near its nest, drenched in pouring rain or menaced by fire and smoke, and this feeling frightened her. She was evidently the only one who felt this way, she and Mr. Rappaport-Lieben, because Mr. Herman Cohen still preferred to be patient, to wait and see what would happen when they reached the port of embarkation. He had gone so far in his imagination that he projected himself through the whole trip, and impelled by a feeling of responsibility to do his best as intermediary and interpreter, he was thinking about the port and the ship and about what would happen next. Mr. Brenske had told them at the camp that they were like enemy soldiers who had been taken captive and this was the way they were being treated. Even now this fact gave the guards the right to be strict and vigilant though everything was absolutely calm. As long as no one needed to go into the last compartment, where the two toilets were, nothing stirred in the train except for its diligent, hurrying wheels as they ran along the tracks.

Mr. Herman Cohen was adding up what their exchange

had cost so far and he eventually arrived at the final sum. He thought about a lot of other things, among them that some of this money might be charged to the United States government, considering how it had stalled and hesitated before agreeing to ransom them. He thought back on all that had happened since they had been captured, as though he was capable only now of grasping it and adding up the cost. He also pondered over the mental and physical condition of the other nineteen gentlemen. Facing his two mute guards, he told himself that they had been able to buy back their lives because they could afford it. But there were millions of other people who didn't even have enough money to die. This was fair and unfair too—and, after all, in helping Katerina Horovitzova, he'd done more than any of the others. He put this down on the credit side of his conscience.

Mr. Cohen examined his conscience briefly.

Why did Mr. Rappaport-Lieben always get so upset about everything? With all his experience in battling through life, Herman Cohen certainly had no illusions either, but here they were on the train and here were their passports too. They were all citizens of a great country and they had plenty of money. This meant something to the Reich, whether or not it was openly admitted, and Mr. Brenske had said as much. The truth was that everybody was suspicious and expected some sort of trickery, but at least for the time being there had been none. Aside from the unexpected sums of money they had been asked to pay. Who, if they were in a position like Mr. Brenske's and had any sense at all, wouldn't want to exchange their prisoners and make money on it at the same time? Everybody knows that two and two make four. Mr. Cohen tried to understand Friedrich Brenske, no matter how much he despised him. The idea of their being "captive enemy soldiers" was really rather flattering.

That amiable phrase about being among the lucky ones echoed in Herman Cohen's memory along with the sound of Mr. Brenske's voice as he'd said it. And his frosty smile. It depressed him to remember, but then he pulled himself together. The distrust and suspicion which he felt about everything was certainly because of the camp and because of the tailor, who had looked so miserable. Suddenly the word "camp" seemed hardly enough to describe it. Why, it had been a whole city; he would have almost said it was a whole world in itself if he had not seen for himself that there were better parts of the world where there were no camps like this one . . . yet. That little adverb nagged at him. Each of them had behaved so differently—Mr. Friedrich Brenske on the one hand and, in contrast, the loutish Corporal Emerich Vogeltanz.

He needed to talk to someone, so he tried to start up a conversation with the guards. "Gentlemen . . ." They remained silent. He asked to speak to Mr. Brenske. Still no response. The wheels of the train rolled on, playing their march with startling clarity.

Even though he had to use his imagination because of the blackout, he could feel how the night had cleansed everything away.

I won't forget this evening for a long, long time, Herman Cohen said to himself. None of the nineteen gentlemen would probably have any objections if he should suggest that they form a club, once they were safely on the other side. The idea appealed to Mr. Cohen. There are some moments which you keep coming back to all your life. You can't help it.

Camp and *sundown,* the wheels kept hammering into the iron rails. The same thing, over and over again.

"It's stuffy in here," Mr. Cohen told the guards. "Couldn't we open the window a little bit?" Still nobody said anything. So it stayed just as stuffy as ever in the compartment.

Katerina Horovitzova was too young to understand all the things which she was feeling, but her fears brought her closer than she realized to the truth. She had matured into the likeness of a woman's body and she felt this and a hundred other things besides in the way the two guards were looking at her as they sat there silently. She wasn't worried by vain attempts to strike up a conversation with them because she hadn't tried. She didn't say it was stuffy in the compartment and she didn't want the window opened. She looked like an illustration in a fashion magazine in her handsome new traveling suit, the black silk blouse she'd chosen, the luxurious underwear which bore the label of a famous Parisian couturier and with the fur coat hanging beside her. Who knows how and from where these things had ended up in the secret division's warehouse? She had never had such a suit before or such underwear or a blouse of silk, but she wore them as though she had always been used to them. She realized that she must go on giving this impression; it was perhaps her only chance. She saw nothing guileful in acting this way, although she sensed it strongly from everything that Mr. Brenske said. She no longer felt like crying because of her family which she'd left behind. Instead, she forced herself to think what she could do so they would be able to come after her. That was why she too finally spoke to her guards, but it didn't do any good in her case either.

Mr. Friedrich Brenske was just coming back from the mail car, where he had sent a telegram to his superior. He opened the door of her compartment.

"I hope I'm not disturbing you," he said.

She was glad the guards were there. For the first time in her life, she was afraid for her body and for her soul. But she hesitated only for a moment.

"I have no idea where we are," she said.

"Let me worry about that, all right?" Mr. Brenske smiled.

She asked if she could have a word with Mr. Cohen, without explaining why or why at that particular moment. When Mr. Brenske asked if he could be present, as though he were paying her a compliment by not asking any reasons, she agreed. A moment later, all three were sitting in Mr. Cohen's compartment. At Mr. Brenske's orders, the guards went out into the corridor. Katerina Horovitzova glanced first at Mr. Herman Cohen, then at Mr. Brenske, and after that she burst out with what was on her mind: would it be possible for Mr. Cohen to ask that her family be allowed to join them?

"It's all I ask," she breathed. "I wouldn't have any reason to go on living without them."

Under normal circumstances, she would probably never have said anything like that. But now it bubbled past her lips by itself. The words rinsed out some of the grief in her heart, but a lot still remained.

"Yes, of course, I understand . . ." said Mr. Brenske. "Who could help but understand you better than I, considering your situation and my own?"

"I'm sure you do," said Mr. Cohen.

"I swear I'd do anything I could to help you."

"Sure, sure," murmured Mr. Herman Cohen. His pale and swollen eyelids blinked several times.

Mr. Brenske looked with new interest at Mr. Herman Cohen. He was obviously thinking over a new possibility.

"Yes, of course, my dear, but it doesn't depend on me," said Mr. Cohen. "We're both of us dependent on Mr. Brenske's good will."

And Mr. Brenske replied gravely that it wasn't even up to him, that he would have to send another telegram.

"I'll see what I can do about it. I'll be back in a minute. But you've said something which made me feel very good," he added as he left. "You said everything depends on good will. Right?" Then Mr. Brenske left the compartment.

Before the guards had resumed their seats, Mr. Herman Cohen kissed Katerina Horovitzova's hand. She accepted it as though she were quite used to having her hand kissed by rich men.

"You shouldn't do that," she said. "No, please . . . I won't know how to repay you for this as long as I live."

"Do you believe in God?" asked Mr. Herman Cohen. "I do."

"I'll start to believe again too."

"Let's not count our chickens before they're hatched. We're in their hands. . . ."

Mr. Brenske's telegram evidently gave him permission to undertake this new operation. He came back beaming.

"It's quite possible and all it needs is one single check to be drawn on your Swiss account. If you agree, we can go right ahead and get down to business. For how many people is this supposed to be?"

Katerina Horovitzova looked at Mr. Cohen.

"Go on, child," he prompted her. "Speak up!"

So she answered Mr. Friedrich Brenske as though she were saying a prayer to both men upon whom everything depended and as though she were also including the silent guards who had come back when Mr. Brenske left and who even now, as they stood in the doorway of the compartment, had not deserted their posts.

"My father, my grandfather, Mother and my six sisters, Sonya, Ludmila, Irena, Eva, Vera and Lea."

"Of course, I can't promise they'll get on the same ship as we will. As it is, we're lucky that we've been given permission to arrange this thing at all. There are certain priorities, of course. But nothing's impossible."

"You must hurry if you want to put Miss Horovitzova's mind at ease," said Herman Cohen.

"Yes, of course, I realize that. That makes a total of nine people, right?" Mr. Brenske remarked. "It'll cost the same amount of money as in your own cases, if that's agreeable to you, and for every additional person who wishes to be exchanged. One hundred thousand gold francs. In one lump sum, of course. All included. I've received instructions from our highest authorities to find out if any of the other gentlemen have relatives in the camp for whom they might wish to arrange an exchange too and if they're willing to pay this ransom, it can be done by telegram so it won't be just one single family. In other words, from one small operation, another one of wider scope can develop. If you look at it this way, another whole ship could be filled up if we don't succeed in getting Miss Horovitzova's family to join us in time. What you would pay in one lump sum, and with a certain loss, would in this case—if we can get a certain number of people—mean more passengers for less money. Like a regular travel agency operates. Only we wouldn't have first and second class. I wish you'd talk this over with the other gentlemen in their compartments."

Mr. Brenske was glowing with zeal. "But time marches on. I must wire back immediately whether you've agreed or not, so no complications will arise back at the camp. Certain plans have been made for all these people. Each one of them has his own fate, so to speak, his place in the scheme of things, his final destination, you might say. Really, in my opinion, the best thing would be if you'd take charge of this yourself. The other gentlemen trust you now. The guards will escort you. This doesn't involve only Miss Horovitzova's family, of course."

As he spoke, Katerina Horovitzova had been watching his lips intently, her eyes brimming with gratitude and uncertainty and devotion in addition to the shy fear she'd shown at first on the ramp. Maybe he wasn't just an adding machine; maybe he really had a heart. She hoped this was true.

"Nine people, not counting me."

"You're already taken care of, though," said Mr. Brenske. "Don't worry about that. I'm the one who's responsible for you in the final calculations. Your family will be exchanged for other individuals independently. You'll have to accept it that way."

Herman Cohen came back from making the rounds of the other compartments, which were decorated with pictures of the Savoy Alps, mountain lakes and chalets. He apologized that his discussions with the other gentlemen had taken so long. Many of them had hesitated; again they were figuring as they had before that they would soon be needing their good money for themselves, as though they had forgotten what they had just gone through and what was still happening. But they were finally convinced that they weren't so safe and sound yet themselves and that Mr. Herman Cohen had given the best example by unselfishly assuring the safety of someone who wasn't even a blood relation. This helped to open other bank accounts. Of course, Mr. Cohen neglected any mention of what Mr. Rappaport-Lieben had said in English (ignoring the presence of the guards): that it was all a lot of filthy blackmail and that neither Mr. Cohen nor the other gentlemen ought to count their chickens before they were hatched, that he'd read *Mein Kampf*. But he finally agreed to pay, like all the rest, for three dozen of his own relatives whom he'd been able to remember in half an hour.

"I'm almost positive," said Mr. Brenske, "that there'll be some additional names they've forgotten the first time and I'd like to hand over a complete list. I hate to trouble you, but after all, you're the spokesman for this group. So I wish you'd go around and talk to them once more. You can count on it that they'll have thought up more names they want to be included. Isn't it amazing how people like you from such a distant land have relatives here and that suddenly you're drawn so close when it's a case of mutual need? Who else could be connected in so many different ways, by so many different threads, as you are?"

Mr. Brenske shook his head as though he were forcing himself to absorb this amazing fact.

Herman Cohen left without another word to Mr.

Brenske and shortly he brought back another list almost as long as the first. The money these names represented was six times the original sum.

"I can see I knew what I was talking about. . . ."

Then Mr. Brenske went off to the mail car. The guards took Katerina Horovitzova back to her compartment and Herman Cohen was left alone again with his silent companions, so he had no opportunity to tell either Mr. Brenske or Katerina Horovitzova what the fussy Mr. Freddy Klarfeld had told him. And he wasn't the only one either, although he was the most explicit. He said that this time it would only be right to pay after the goods had been delivered, so to speak. "It was all right as far as we were concerned. But now? All we'd need to do is to send a bank draft which would only be payable afterward." Mr. Cohen considered whether he ought not to mention this to Mr. Brenske the next time he came around. Everything depended on Mr. Cohen now and he'd never been in a situation quite like this one.

The guards served the first meal. Everybody got a mess tin of boiled barley with water and black coffee. The coffee was cold and a good thirst quencher. They were all satisfied with their meal, especially when they saw that the guards in their compartments had got the same thing. But they took turns so that while one guard was eating, the other was always on the alert and able to suppress a mutiny instantaneously if anybody got the idea. How could Germany ever win the war if this was the kind of stuff they fed their soldiers? Mr. Herman Cohen thought to himself as he downed his mug of coffee almost in one gulp. You can't advance very easily on this amount of calories. It was the first time he had laughed in a long while. Again he remembered what Mr. Klarfeld had said and he finally decided to mention it to Mr. Brenske after all, even though he must find a more tactful way of putting it. But Mr. Brenske didn't come back for a long time. He evidently had a lot of details to clear up in making his final calculations. Later, when Mr. Cohen told him—rather nervously—about the doubts which had been expressed, Mr. Brenske answered curtly.

"No, I don't know why we should change things all of a sudden once they've been agreed on. We're not a couple of haggling little grocery store keepers. You're not and neither am I."

Up until that moment, Mr. Cohen had been burdened with the decision of whether he ought to protest or to admit that Mr. Klarfeld's suggestion was unacceptable so as not to anger Mr. Brenske. He shrugged his shoulders and set aside his untouched tin of barley.

Katerina Horovitzova's coppery golden eyes did not regard her dish of food with nearly as much assurance. She didn't know how to assert herself as well as Mr. Herman Cohen and the others did. They were men, after all. She thought about the money which might already have been paid by now, and about what it represented—the members of her family. It was as though this were a stick gripped firmly in the middle by Mr. Brenske's bony hand. When did this hand strike and when would it give support? Did it ever? Katerina Horovitzova ate her barley and its taste was alloyed with growing misgivings, but it didn't make her any wiser. She ate all the barley, though, down to the last morsel.

Mr. Brenske did not come back again and Herman Cohen turned his thoughts to Katerina Horovitzova, trying to understand her situation, which he had done so much to improve. He realized that her fear was conditioned by the years she and her family had lived here. Much longer than he had. The camp had permeated the whole land and its people, their nerves and souls. That brought him back to where he did not want to be, even in spirit, but he couldn't shake it off. He too belonged to all of it as long as he was here on this dark soil which had been stained by so much blood. It would probably stay with him even over there, when he got to the other side. Again the hammering train wheels penetrated into his consciousness. He wasn't smiling now. Months, years . . . each day. Every hour, every minute, every second. And they, culled out of the mob, were just on the other side of the synagogue walls, walls that breathed cold drafts and names which had ceased to be names anymore. How could the others have found their way through? Now Katerina Horovitzova was no longer alone in his thoughts. People from humbler walks of life have always been more resistant, he thought to himself. This made him feel envious and complacent at the same time, but he pushed away both feelings. He didn't even dare to sigh too loud. His mind turned back to money matters. They'd spent a great deal. Fortunately, there was still a lot left over. He clung to the thought of money, which was like a prop from many sides, still anchored deep enough to hold fast, thank heaven. But was it anchored deep enough, down to where the camp could not reach, down to where the memories of the past began on which he had been weaned? Again he couldn't help feeling sorry for Katerina Horovitzova. It was honest compassion and it took his mind off the misgivings he felt for himself. Happily, the train was still moving at the same speed and there was something inexpressibly therapeutic about this fact.

94

After they had been traveling for about three hours, Mr. Brenske came back to Katerina Horovitzova's compartment. He was wearing his fine new suit. He apologized for coming to her to ask for an additional large sum of money to cover additional expenses connected with everybody's relatives, including her own family. He said he realized that she wasn't the person who was going to pay, but he would appreciate it if she would go with him and ask Mr. Herman Cohen for the money herself. Then he quoted a figure which made chills run up her spine.

"You see, I realize—and I hope you understand me, Miss Horovitzova—how hard it is for people to part with their money, particularly people who know better than anyone else how much their money can buy and how much pleasure it can bring. Not everybody has the right outlook on this. We see eye to eye about it and I'm counting on you. In other words, you always hit a snag when you want money from people who have a lot of it, the worst kind of snag, as I've seen for myself. But there are more reasons for paying this money than anyone might think. There are unexpected expenditures here for the guards, the train, fuel, postal services and so on. For everything, to make a long story short. And finally there's the ship. I have an idea that you yourself come from a family of modest means. I'd even go so far as to say you're from a poor family. At least I've pieced this together from the information I've received so far about your relatives. Apparently the only property you left to our Warsaw fund were two foot-powered wood lathes. People like your folks have had to work hard to make a living. But most of them never realize what money's worth really. I believe both lathes are being donated by your father and grandfather to raise money for their trip.

This is in addition to the large sum I mentioned first, which isn't coming out of their pockets. I hope you'll soon be together again. Just wait and see."

In his civilian clothes, he seemed almost feverish with excitement as they neared the port of embarkation. The next leg of their trip would be by sea. There was a sudden and unusual haste, as though there was still a lot to be done and he didn't want to let things get out of control.

"You have no idea to what extent the final calculations depend on the success of what I've been explaining to you and how the success of the operation now under way is dependent on this too," he said. Katerina Horovitzova was tortured with misgivings, wondering whether even such a lot of money could pay for so many people, and she wondered whether what had already happened would not perhaps be put in jeopardy. Silently she accompanied Mr. Brenske into the next compartment and smiled meekly at Mr. Herman Cohen. He seemed surprised by the request and almost offended, as though he had had some doubts himself about the other gentlemen. He recalled Mr. Klarfeld's remark. It took a little while before half of them had signed their checks. Mr. Freddy Klarfeld raised the same objections as before.

This time, speaking for himself, Mr. Cohen said, "We're not small-town grocers, to haggle this way. You certainly must be able to see what's going on and what's involved. We aren't at the stock market or in some democratic legislature."

Nevertheless, some of the men still refused their signatures.

"How much money are we still worth?" they demanded.

Again it was only the example of the others and especially of Mr. Cohen which won them over.

"Can we afford this?" queried Mr. Siretzsky.

A few of the gentlemen added a clause below their signature, noting that "Remainder will be paid after delivery."

Mr. Cohen considered for a moment and then he went back to Mr. Brenske. But before he handed over the checks, he said something to Katerina Horovitzova that he'd wanted to say for a long time. He assured her that once they were out of this mess, she'd surely be able to find an excellent job at Mr. Rappaport-Lieben's nightclub. "It's called the Gondola, which is a kind of boat. Only it's Mr. Brenske and his superiors who are holding the rudder right now, not us. But afterward you'll be at the rudder yourself. You're still young and you've got your whole life in front of you."

She smiled almost warmly, not sure that this really concerned her. "As my grandfather used to say, may God give you a golden tongue," she told Mr. Cohen.

What had Mr. Brenske meant by telling her about those two lathes which had stayed in their apartment?

Then Mr. Cohen ventured to ask Mr. Brenske whether, in keeping with commercial custom and in order to reassure some of the other gentlemen ("I don't want to mention any names," he said), who had shown a certain impatience, at least part of the additional final payment could not be made after the deal was satisfactorily concluded. The guarantees were there in their legally valid signatures.

Mr. Brenske frowned. "I thought I was dealing with men who have seen and understand the world," he said bluntly. "Up till now, I have gotten a certain impression of high ethical standards from you as people, I don't mind telling you. On my desk I have receipts bearing the official stamp of our Reich for every expenditure which has been made so far. I don't know why something that is as clear as day need be made so complicated by tacking on all sorts of conditions. We're not partners who have come into the world to ask a lot of favors, even though we don't belong on your ladder of plutocracy. I've got a perfect right to say this, you realize that. But I won't rub salt into the wounds which, I'm sorry to see, are still open between us. . . . Our Reich picked you out of the mob of other prisoners. It made up a special train for you, arranged for you to be exchanged and so determined your fate. The coaches you're riding in belong to a special train reserved for very important people. Some of the men who are guarding you are members of the Reich Honor Guard. I was made responsible for you even though I had plenty of other, more important things to do. With all modesty, I have every right to take exception to your attitude. I think I would have good reason to feel offended. There are millions of people in the mother camp and its affiliated camps who would like to be in your shoes. I can't go on with this assignment unless I have your confidence. Your attitude even casts a shadow on those who do trust me. Make up your mind, please. Tell the rest of your people who haven't signed yet what I've told you. But make up your minds quickly, without any strings attached."

Mr. Brenske went out, looking deeply irritated. Now they must make up their minds. He came back shortly, looking just as curt and cross as he had before. This time, Mr. Cohen didn't even have a chance to report that the rest of the gentlemen had agreed. It turned out now that Mr. Brenske had a new demand, in addition to the original condition. First, Mr. Cohen and the other nineteen gentlemen were to pay one million gold francs as a fine for the delay, which had caused great loss to the Reich because this money had been counted on. Secondly, they must pay another million francs for the ship, which had to be insured for this amount if the exchange was still to be carried through. In the third place—and this concerned only Mr. Cohen and Katerina Horovitzova—they should kindly take note of certain unforeseeable circumstances which had arisen because of the last cable. Coldness emanated from him and Mr. Cohen suddenly went limp.

"Did you hear what I said?"

"No," said Mr. Cohen. "Not . . . not exactly." But he had heard every word quite clearly and he was ready to agree to almost anything.

"Sir," Mr. Brenske said suddenly, his tone gentler than his expression, "believe me, I sometimes have the feeling that this whole exchange operation is beyond me. I know you've got money, but I know too that you've got other ways to invest it. You're people who aim toward some specific goal and you have no time for the unpredictable. I hate to introduce any elements of discord into this. But I'd like to quote one of our German authors, who wrote that some people think they're going to set the world on fire, yet not even dogs care enough to bark at them. Nobody can ever be completely sure of anything. I can't, and neither can you. So . . ."

Mr. Brenske took a deep breath and continued. "That is why I'm asking you to understand all the explanations I've given you—and you in particular ought to show a special amount of understanding—and remember that I'm not the one who decides these things and there's nothing I can do to change them. But it turns out that every delay on your part is costing too much, so some people are beginning to get disturbed because they see that in the meantime our losses are mounting too."

"What are you getting at?" Mr. Herman Cohen asked nervously. "I hope this doesn't mean that complications have come up?" He didn't understand why Mr. Brenske had brought Katerina Horovitzova into his compartment to hear him say this.

"Well," said Mr. Brenske, "as far as you and Miss Horovitzova are concerned, the unfortunate fact is that your authorities have refused to include her in your passport and so the new travel certificate is not valid. On account of all this red tape, it looks as though she'll have to wait and come with the next transport."

Katerina Horovitzova stiffened.

"I don't know to what extent it's important that you leave together, but I don't know what else to suggest," Mr. Brenske went on in a rueful tone. "Your authorities obviously don't believe us. Perhaps they suspect we're up to something because of Katerina Horovitzova. This is just another example of how our enemies inside your country and elsewhere overseas have vilified us, how they smear us and incite people against us. We've already indicated that she's a dancer without much experience, too young to be involved in the sort of activities they seem to have in mind."

"I thought it all depended on you," said Herman Cohen.

"Only up to a certain point," replied Mr. Brenske. "She's a citizen of the General Government, a former Pole, in other words a citizen of ours, and your authorities haven't expressed themselves very favorably, even taking into consideration their usual curt behavior. We've been informed that the whole thing would be possible if you were married. They evidently assume you know whom you want to marry. You're the only one in your group who isn't married. But for reasons of racial purity, our authorities are not permitted to perform a wedding ceremony for a couple like you. It's a very strict regulation and I don't know whether you'd even want to do it this way. . . ."

Mr. Brenske had once told his subordinate, Lieutenant Schillinger, that from his experience, whenever you want to tell someone a special lie, you must always look him unflinchingly in the eye. This gives an impression of innocence and candor. But he also mentioned that you must choose just the right person for it.

"You're a widower, I believe."

And Mr. Brenske sighed again, as though this fact made him even sadder. He looked as though he were making a silent plea for help and understanding.

"Of course, I'd certainly be willing. It's only *pro forma*, after all, and I'm sure Miss Horovitzova would agree too."

"Yes . . ." said Katerina Horovitzova. "I'd be willing . . . I wouldn't even . . . say no . . . to the other alternative."

"As far as I'm concerned, if I were to advise you, the second alternative might take a long time," Mr. Brenske said stiffly. "But do as you like, of course. Everybody engineers his own fate. There's just so much that we can do and no more."

"Well, then, if it's all right with Mr. Cohen . . . I'd be . . . grateful," said Katerina Horovitzova meekly.

"Then that just leaves us with the question of the wedding. It would have to be performed back at the camp. As I told you, it's out of the question anywhere else."

"But we're not lepers," objected Herman Cohen.

"I didn't say you were," Mr. Brenske replied. "But rules are rules and this holds true all over our country."

"We're not one bit worse than anybody else."

"It's a law, you see, and no matter what kind of a law it is, we must respect it. We are citizens of this country and you are foreigners. There's nothing to be done about it; you just aren't our kind of people."

"Can't it be done outside the camp?" asked Herman Cohen.

"Practically speaking, it's out of the question for you today anywhere but in a camp," Mr. Brenske said and added, "All this will delay us, of course, and increase the cost. The train will have to turn back right away—which is another problem—because while we're talking, we are headed toward your port of embarkation. This indecision drags things on even longer."

"All right, do what you think best," said Mr. Cohen.

He glanced at Katerina Horovitzova and he knew that if he hesitated now, he would betray himself and his conscience. Katerina Horovitzova's fate hung by a hair for one split second. But he was frightened by the darkness in his soul and he rapidly pushed aside all his doubts. Now there was no other way.

"Do you want to do it without the knowledge of the other gentlemen?" asked Mr. Brenske. "Or do you simply want to let them know through the guards so they won't get upset when we turn around and go back? It can be done either way, but as you can see, it's complicated and means a lot more work." Mr. Brenske implied that he was doing all this on his own initiative.

"All right then, you do whichever you wish to do," Herman Cohen said heavily. And then he signed another check. He didn't even have time to add this up in his mind to the total amount they'd paid already. He did it only after the guard in the corridor had taken Katerina Horovitzova back to her own compartment. He was glad that he had signed the check on behalf of all the others. They might have hesitated to sign checks themselves.

"Thank you," said Mr. Brenske brusquely. "There's such a lot of arranging to be done, I hardly know what to do first. I'll have a receipt for this stamped and certified immediately. Every penny is carefully recorded and nothing's gone astray. You won't find a single error when it comes to the final settlement."

On their way back to the camp, neither Mr. Cohen nor the others saw Mr. Brenske. Mr. Cohen was glad he was alone in his compartment so he didn't have to explain to the others why they were going in the opposite direction. Some of the gentlemen didn't even notice it because of the blackout. They thought the train had been shifted onto a different track at one of the stations along the way. But after a while, Mr. Friedrich Brenske himself announced the fact on behalf of Mr. Cohen. Suddenly they stopped and there was the camp next to the ramp again. At the station, Mr. Brenske told them it wasn't morning yet, only daybreak, that they were back at the mother camp and that they must make haste with the ceremony so they could be back at the port again before the next blackout. "We need the dusk, fog and night for this exchange operation, so we're covered," he explained. "It's going to cost each of you gentlemen one thousand gold francs and an additional one thousand dollars in a lump sum for the whole group because that's what it costs to postpone a ship's sailing in any seaport, even a second-rate place like Haiti or Havana, not to mention at docks which require high-caliber antiaircraft installations and a high degree of fire-fighting readiness. It's not such an awful lot of money this time and I'm sure you'll pay up. All the receipts for the final settlement have been prepared for you. If I didn't really have to, I wouldn't come to you with any more requests of any kind."

"Then I can invite my parents?" asked Katerina Horovitzova with misgivings.

"Yes, of course. What kind of a wedding would it be without the parents of the bride? Even though we all realize that this time the wedding's just for the sake of appearances. So you can leave. But I've heard that they're handing over their wood lathes right now in another part of the camp, so maybe it won't be very easy to find them. Well, don't worry. But first, we must find the proper person who will perform this wedding with all the blessings of your race and faith."

"All right," said Mr. Cohen.

They felt uncomfortable to be back at the camp again. They were not reassured either by the way Mr. Brenske kept describing it as the "mother camp." Mr. Taubenstock and Mr. Rauchenberg clutched their passports inside their pockets and Mr. Samuel Landau and Mr. Leo Rubin looked at Mr. Cohen almost resentfully, as though he were to blame for their being here again. Some of the gentlemen stared at Katerina Horovitzova. She could read their thoughts and inwardly she apologized to all of them as tears welled in her eyes.

"For the time being, gentlemen, no one may leave his place," Mr. Brenske called down the corridors of the two coaches. "And since you've already been cleared and released once from the mother camp, no one may go outside either. This decision is final and it is not open to appeal."

He ordered the guards to open the doors, which wasn't necessary because everyone had heard his announcement in German the first time and then in translation. A voice called out from Mr. Rappaport-Lieben's compartment: "I'm not going to pay a single franc more! I've had enough of all this trickery!"

That was tactless. Everybody was thinking about the wedding.

"Now that we're here, if any of you gentlemen would like to stay in exchange for one of the relatives on your list, this can easily be arranged. But I'll have to know right away on account of the number of places on the ship."

"I'm not giving one more penny and I want to get out of here, if this railroad really leads anywhere," Mr. Rappaport-Lieben went on shouting, while alone in his compartment Mr. Herman Cohen made out a check for the proper amount in the name of Mr. Rappaport-Lieben.

"This isn't how it was supposed to have been," Mr. Rappaport-Lieben called from his compartment. But despite all his courage, he was still too scared to stick his head out of the compartment door while the German guards were there. "Why, we're beggars by now anyway!" he added.

"Doesn't Mr. Rappaport-Lieben have any relatives who could help him out if the need arose?" Mr. Brenske asked Mr. Herman Cohen pityingly.

"Of course he does," Mr. Cohen answered firmly and almost irritably. "We've all got relatives like that. There's no need to get discouraged on account of a couple of dollars when we've paid out as much as we already have."

He meant it ambiguously, but this was lost on Mr. Brenske. He gave permission for the blackout curtains to be raised so all the gentlemen saw the camp stretching out on both sides of the tracks as night lifted and dawn came. They saw the thick smoke rising from the chimneys and people dressed like the tailor yesterday in the synagogue. There were a lot of soldiers in frog-green uniforms and men with machine guns in the towers. Yesterday they had not been able to notice all this in detail.

The first thing Mr. Rappaport-Lieben saw was how right next to the train a soldier shot a woman by the barbed-wire fence, and Mr. Leo Rubin couldn't believe his eyes as he watched two young soldiers playing tug-of-war with a little child until it was torn asunder.

"This is terrible!" shrieked Mr. Rappaport-Lieben. "What's going on here?"

"We've been fooled," he kept saying. At home, he sometimes used to go to inspect his stockyards and look through the fence at the herds of cattle, all of which had been brought there simply to be slaughtered. None of them ever escaped.

"But we ought to have a chance to talk directly with whoever's in charge here!" Mr. Lowenstein insisted.

"I guess I'd better have the window shades pulled down," said Mr. Brenske, ignoring the last remark. "I have no idea what's going on. I'll investigate myself and see the proper punishment is given."

He went outside briefly and came right back.

Mr. Lowenstein again requested a word with the representative of the International Red Cross, even though it was clear that by doing this, he was making it quite obvious that his personal confidence in Mr. Friedrich Brenske's promises was diminishing and also, indirectly, his trust in the others too. Just like Mr. Rappaport-Lieben. And he was doing it now while they were on camp territory and about to receive a written receipt for all the money they had paid out. Mr. Brenske had also promised them an explanation of what was going on outside.

"Well, I'm afraid it's impossible here," Mr. Brenske replied promptly. "I'll tell you that quite candidly, and I'm just sorry I must keep repeating things I've already explained before. This territory around here is exclusively our domain and it is governed by military regulations. You must realize this yourselves, gentlemen, and see that it's just impossible, even if I might be willing to wink my eye. What if later this representative whom one of you wants to talk to were to abuse our good will and the fact that we've invited him to come here? Even though I mentioned a need for confidence on your part, I must speak frankly and tell you that our side feels a certain amount of distrust toward you. It involves other cases on a higher level, offenses of national significance in which the outlook of one individual doesn't mean very much. I'm really sorry I've got to keep telling you this all the time."

It was a drizzly morning in mid-September and Mr. Brenske said that what had happened outside had been just a misunderstanding. At the same time, he asked whether the proper sum had already been signed for, because he had just found out from a special dispatch that the number of German war prisoners selected for exchange had been cut down by half and in order to even things up, an additional one million gold Swiss francs must be paid.

"I feel like a bank clerk and not like a soldier," Mr. Brenske complained. "It almost goes against my grain. Fortunately, you've got the money and believe me, I sometimes envy you, the way it helps you through all kinds of tight squeezes. From now on, I'd like to be able to tell you only pleasant things and I have a feeling that it won't be long, as long as the decision to go ahead won't have to be changed for military reasons. But this puts my mind at ease. I mean, what I was telling you, that this will really be the last request we'll have to make of you. I've got all your receipts right here in my hand. Actually, the last request wasn't because of us. It wasn't in our power to foresee the unforeseeable. I deeply admire correct behavior and that's why I tell you this. It just can't be helped, gentlemen. If you want to make up for the smaller number of German war prisoners offered now by your authorities for exchange, you've got to pay for the difference."

And so the rest of the gentlemen, who, like Mr. Lowenstein, Mr. Rubin and Mr. Rappaport-Lieben, had just seen the camp through the train windows, reached for their fountain pens and wrote their checks.

Mr. Otto Rauchenberg peered with his narrowed blue eyes through his gold-rimmed glasses at the drawn window blind and didn't say a word, just as he'd sat all the way to the camp the first time, all the way to the port and back again. The smoke gobbled up the light as day broke and the train stood immobile. It was an uncomfortable kind of immobility; they all sat there in something like a state of shock.

"I'll arrange everything so you won't have to stay here any longer than necessary," said Mr. Brenske, as though he had read their thoughts. "You may move around freely," he went on. "Just inside, of course. Don't try to leave the train. For your own good."

All nineteen gentlemen instantly hurried to Mr. Herman

Cohen's compartment. Mute questions were directed to him and to each other; eyebrows and chins, eyeballs and arms waggled in the direction of the camp, but no one said a word because the guards were still there. Smoke was everywhere and the people outside moved like shadows of the machine gun towers. Mr. Rappaport-Lieben began to weep.

"I've seen the death of thousands of cows and heifers and steers. . . . I know what it is. . . ."

"Quit your sniveling."

"For God's sake, don't attract any more attention to us!"

"Pull yourself together."

"They have no idea back home . . ."

"I've got a family, children. . . ."

"We've still got a chance."

"Not much, but some, perhaps."

"This wasn't the fault of any one of us."

"We should have just looked out for ourselves."

"We won't be able to pay for this even with our blood."

"Let's not get all demoralized."

"Let's wait and see what'll happen."

"Plenty!"

"No wedding, no funeral . . . nothing."

"Look, we've still got a lot of money, they know this very well, and that gives us not only a chance," said Mr. Herman Cohen loudly, "but also a sense of confidence. Let's sit tight and stand fast. After all, we're people of status."

But Mr. Rappaport-Lieben kept on sighing.

"The stockyards . . . thousands of steers . . . money, dignity, and at the end, there was always blood. . . ."

Mr. Rauchenberg kept staring at the window blind but his eyes saw nothing more than what had happened outside that window when they'd raised the blind. Suddenly his gold-rimmed glasses slipped off and it looked as if he stepped on them accidentally; the glass splintered. But he didn't say a word about it to anyone.

The train had been standing in the station for quite some time and the heating system had stopped working. Everybody was cold, even Mr. Herman Cohen.

Katerina Horovitzova bundled herself up in the fur coat. She was embarrassed that some of the recriminations were against her, that she was to blame for their return, for the fact that they were shivering there on the siding. Now she too realized what Mr. Rappaport-Lieben already understood.

In the meantime, so there would be no repetition of what he had called a "misunderstanding," Mr. Brenske had the area within sight of the train cleared away and then he summoned Rabbi Dajem from Lodz, who worked in the hair-drying room next to the third oven. He was to perform the wedding ceremony. When he came, the gentlemen were somewhat reassured, though Mr. Rappaport-Lieben kept talking about the stockyards. The others shifted their attention to the old man.

"Go right ahead as though there weren't any war going on. Just remember you mustn't get out of the train if you've already been subtracted from the total number," said Mr. Brenske.

"You want it with prayer?" asked Rabbi Dajem, surprised, as though it could have been done any other way.

"I told you, as though we weren't at war. We want the proper kind of wedding. Is this compartment big enough?"

Rabbi Dajem looked down the length of the coach, pausing at each face to study it briefly. He nodded at the short-sighted squint of Mr. Otto Rauchenberg and the tears of Rappaport-Lieben and finally his eyes came to rest on Katerina Horovitzova.

"So you're the one it's supposed to be, my lonesome soul."

And he caressed her cheek with special gentleness. "Like a peach, like a flower. My dear little thing," he said, "I know, I know," he went on, as though he were talking to himself. "Your mother won't be at your wedding and your father won't either and neither will your grandfather and your six sisters. My little unjust one . . . do you think it's right, what you're doing, when even here there's no one to whom you bow your knee? No, don't kneel down . . . stand up."

Mr. Brenske let him talk and smiled frostily.

"But now let's get down to business and not talk so much, all right?" he interrupted in a jocular tone. "What do you need for your ceremony? Wine? I'll have some wine brought. Ritual articles for your ceremony? We've got so much of that stuff, you'd be able to perform marriage ceremonies for all your men and women from now until Judgment Day. And every day is Judgment Day here, isn't it, Rabbi?"

Rabbi Dajem from Lodz nodded. "After all, in the last analysis isn't it God alone who guides our steps, no matter where we go, no matter where we stand, no matter where we kneel and where we die?" he asked. "Isn't He, after all, despite everything, omnipresent, invisible and supremely just?"

Katerina Horovitzova gazed at the old man and sought an answer to the question which glimmered in her as it had yesterday when the tailor had looked into her eyes.

"Our devotion to Him is everlasting."

"I asked if my family would be allowed to come," Katerina Horovitzova said suddenly to Mr. Brenske.

"Yes, I asked that they be here, but apparently they're in the disinfection station because of their next assignment. And we're in somewhat of a hurry. That is, to a certain extent, we are pressed for time because we don't want to miss another sundown. And then, too, your wedding is just a formality, so to speak. The whole thing is being done so the proper papers can be drawn up and you can be put into Herman Cohen's passport."

"Can we put up the window shades?" asked Katerina Horovitzova.

"Ah, my evil little one, my foolish child," said Rabbi Dajem of Lodz as he stroked her hair. "Don't ask for that."

"All right, now, let's get going," urged Mr. Brenske sternly.

The old man made the preparations for the ceremony, but no one could understand very well what he was singing about. Perhaps that was because the other nineteen gentlemen with the American passports, not to mention Mr. Herman Cohen, were all rather nervous. It was as though they could look through the drawn window shades out onto the flat plains which lay beyond the streets of the camp. Fence posts and wires ran off into the distance, into infinity. Ramps and railroad tracks ran like threads of silver and clay as far as the eye could see.

"I'll be a witness and so will the guards, if that's possible in your religion," Mr. Brenske offered charitably. "I don't think anyone will accuse me of anything disgraceful if I'm doing this just as a matter of form, like the two of you and everybody else," he added.

"Ah, my last little survivor," the old man murmured indistinctly. "Once alight and a thousand times extinguished."

"Come on, come on, you've got to hurry with this sort of thing, too, sometimes," Mr. Brenske said, again in a jocular tone.

Then the old man talked about the ancient wedding theme, about the evil inclination which is almost always stronger than the power to resist it, and about the bond between man and woman which is guided by the all-wise ruler of the world, by whose word the universe was created and the sun and the moon and the countless stars, and then he spoke of love and affection, of fidelity and devotion, and about how under all circumstances and conditions, in every eventuality, Katerina Horovitzova and Herman Cohen should stand by each other and never leave each other.

"Well, aren't you going to sing?" Mr. Brenske interrupted the old man.

"Extinguished a thousand times," the old man repeated.

The rabbi's chants sounded more like a funeral than a wedding, but no one felt like asking why and Mr. Rappaport-Lieben began to shout again.

"We're like a herd of cattle!"

Then Rabbi Dajem of Lodz stood to one side, ignoring Mr. Rappaport-Lieben just as he had ignored Mr. Brenske, and he went on singing, keeping one hand against the blackout curtain over the compartment window in case one of the gentlemen might suddenly try to force it open. With the other hand, he pronounced a benediction over Katerina Horovitzova's head. She was afraid she knew why he was singing the chant for the dead.

"First and last," he said. "Fog and night and fog and fire."

From his words, she also understood the meaning of the text "I went forth," which he repeated several times, and she understood him when he said just the opposite, "Do not leave." And she trembled.

Then he said something she could understand a little better, about entering the Holy of Holies and about the springs of Eden. She was pale as a proxy bride as she kissed Mr. Herman Cohen on the lips for the first time, as is required in Jewish weddings.

"All right, now, get back where you came from, songbird. Don't hold up our departure. We're late enough as it is," Mr. Brenske said suddenly and nodded to the guards to take care of Rabbi Dajem from Lodz and escort him off the train. "That didn't take so long. No need to lose any more time. Well, here we go again."

The old man with his pastoral blue eyes, dressed in prison clothes, had married Katerina Horovitzova and Herman Cohen just so she could be put on his passport. Rabbi Dajem was still singing. He stood close beside her until the guards seized him under his arms, one on each side. But he kept on singing, paying no attention to anybody else, as though this was what Mr. Brenske had ordered him to do. Aside from the moment when he had caressed Katerina Horovitzova's hair, he gave the impression that he was out of his mind.

"I'll pray for you, my little lamb," he said. "I'm the boss in the hair-drying room, my lovely one, and your hair's so shiny and silky. Like black satin. My other little lambs are waiting for me over there and I must hurry back to them, because they're leaving me and they don't want to go. First and Last and Last and First, One and Only, One and Only. If they don't run away from me, I won't run away from them, and you won't either, my strong young child. Not even you, my poor, unhappy one, my poor, dear, grieving little one."

Mr. Brenske slapped him on the back like a horse. It looked odd, but apparently there wasn't anything strange about it. The old man seemed used to it. He went away, like one of a herd of cattle, stupidly and without any will of his own, just as Mr. Rappaport-Lieben had said at first.

The adjutant brought another dispatch into the compartment for Mr. Brenske and it turned out that now there was something else to pay for. Mr. Brenske stared at the wire in eloquent silence. Maybe he was really embarrassed by now and didn't want to show it.

"We must be strong," he said. "Next time, though, I'll send back a personal appeal."

Mr. Rappaport-Lieben shouted that he wasn't going to stand for this anymore and that he didn't have bugs in his brain, that the whole business with the rabbi was just an act and that he insisted on leaving immediately.

"Either or!" he bellowed. "Not even the robber barons in the Middle Ages behaved this way! You've made us into beggars. What more do you want?"

"Is that all Mr. Rappaport-Lieben suspects us of?" Mr. Brenske asked, suddenly calm and matter-of-fact, as if it was only his own words that gave him back his sense of dignity. "I happen to know a little bit about ancient history. I know what happened in Persia and along the valleys of the Rhine and the Danube and the Don. Why, I know the history of usury too. I don't want to pass judgment on who was guilty of what in the past or toss a coin to find out who's innocent.

But first of all, I can't agree with you. We simply have different opinions about it."

Mr. Vladimir Arnstein from Odessa and Mr. Hans Adler from New York grabbed Mr. Rappaport-Lieben's elbows.

"What's that smoke coming out of those chimneys? What kind of factories are they?" shrieked Rappaport-Lieben, and the mood of the wedding and Mr. Brenske's conciliatory and august words were forgotten for good.

"Mr. Rappaport-Lieben . . ."

Katerina Horovitzova stood there like a culprit.

Suddenly there was a new tension. Nobody knew what the young woman was going to do. But Herman Cohen pulled out his fountain pen and signed a check. Now it was possible to leave in time for them to be at the port before twilight—as Mr. Brenske reminded them again—so they could finally embark.

"Your papers will be ready during the course of the trip. We won't stay here any longer," he added and smiled like someone who is doing a harder job than anyone might realize. "Everything points almost without an obstacle to the goal we've set for ourselves."

Then each of the gentlemen received a carefully itemized list of his expenditures for his individual ransom.

The train pulled away from the loading platform of the camp, its curtains drawn for the blackout. Katerina Horovitzova sat almost without moving during the entire eight hours of their trip. Mr. Herman Cohen did not say a word to her the whole time. They had been allowed to sit together, in the presence of the guards.

Before it got dark that evening, Mr. Friedrich Brenske came back and told them that they had reached the Hanseatic city of Hamburg. Perhaps they could hear the sea?

"An old and glorious German city," he said. "You see, we've kept our promise. And we will, right down to the last detail. Now you can see the sea. . . ."

He had the guards raise the blackout curtain and there beside the wharf Katerina Horovitzova and Mr. Herman Cohen saw a big ship rocking at anchor. The *Deutschland.*

"Just wait and see how embarrassed our doubting Thomases will be," said Mr. Brenske.

"The ship," said Mr. Cohen briefly.

Then Katerina Horovitzova kissed Herman Cohen on the lips again, as she had kissed the tailor the day before. The same words were echoed in many tongues, twenty times, a hundred, perhaps a thousand times, as the window shades were raised in each compartment: "the ship," "port," "the sea," "voyage," "the end," "the beginning."

"Oh, how I wish Mother were here! And my father and grandfather and my sisters," sighed Katerina Horovitzova, more moved and excited than ever.

"They'll be just as thrilled as you are," Mr. Brenske remarked and almost smiled in gratification. He always looked people straight in the eye when he spoke to them. "We want everything to go smoothly. I play fair and square. Will you ask the others to come in here?" Mr. Brenske said to the guards.

Mr. Brenske didn't begin until they had all entered the compartment, one after the other, almost in alphabetical order, just like the evening before when they'd boarded the train at sundown as their names were called from the list: Mr. Adler, Mr. Arnstein, Mr. Bettelheim, Mr. Ekstein, Mr. Gerstl, Mr. Ginsburg, Mr. Klarfeld, Mr. Landau, Mr. Lowenstein, Mr. Rauchenberg, Mr. Raven, Mr. Rubin, Mr. Taubenstock, Mr. Schnurdreher, Mr. Siretzsky, Mr. Vaksman, Mr. Varecky, Mr. Zweig and finally Mr. Rappaport-Lieben, who stood in the doorway. Then Mr. Brenske began to speak.

"I have one final request to make of you. Perhaps you can guess what it is and because, in your way, you're exceptional people, I'm afraid you'll have some objections to what I'm going to ask and perhaps even some counterconditions which could jeopardize this whole operation just as it is about to be brought to a successful conclusion. I want to stress right at the start that this is our very last request and our highest authorities stand behind it. This operation is almost over. There's a certain sum of gold francs which we need so that this ship you see over there can get under way. Maybe you don't have this much money yourselves—nobody has any intention of asking you for more than you can afford—but your relatives have money. We know you have influential brothers or wives and many of you already have grown-up children with positions of their own. I'm kind of tired by now, so please excuse me for being so brief. Secondly, we hope you'll write to your relatives abroad and tell them how decently we've treated you. I might as well be quite honest with you; leading individuals in our country, persons in the very highest places, put a great deal of importance on what kind of letters you will write and whether they will show a sufficient amount of gratitude. I'll tell you frankly, this affair of ours is winding up and there's no time to waste. What we don't do now won't get done. That's why I'm putting first things first. These letters of yours will be sent to your country by special courier. Write them as you see fit, but I would advise you to write them in such a way that they describe all the generosity with which we've treated you. Nothing else is involved, except remembering what possibilities we have. So the deepest-dyed pessimists will have to keep their mouths shut. Of course, we can't force you to do this and it wouldn't be ethical either. We hope you'll do it by yourselves. Look what a fine ship is waiting for you there!"

Mr. Bettelheim's eyes grew misty. The sight of the ship had moved him to tears.

"Look out there at the sea, which is all ready to bear this vessel to the destination that has been set for it by you and by us. The end of the voyage is no longer out of sight. The text of the telegrams to your relatives about this final sum of money is included among the papers which the guards will distribute among you. I suggest you don't take too long about this. Just as your authorities have been hard-nosed and intransigent, especially about including one of our important army officers in the exchange quota, so our higher authorities—in retaliation—are becoming increasingly firm. So that's why, for the third time, I'm asking you to pay up and write your letters."

The guards distributed to every person a sheet of paper and an envelope, each a different color or at least a different tint.

"What do you think we are? You think we've gone out of our heads or what?" shouted Mr. Rappaport-Lieben, but Mr. Klarfeld and Mr. Landau yelled something at him sharply so Mr. Brenske passed over it as though nothing had happened.

"You may go back to your compartments now and write your letters."

Everybody wrote a letter except for Rappaport-Lieben, who was white as chalk, and Katerina Horovitzova, who had no one to write to because all her family was dead by now. In her memory, she turned back to Rabbi Dajem of Lodz, seeking something in his words, and what she found was almost identical with what Rappaport-Lieben had discovered or suspected.

He was howling from his compartment again. "It's a fraud! It's a disgusting, charlatan fake! Nobody will even put his toe on board that ship alive! Nobody'll be able to stick his little finger or even his fingernail in the sea and nobody's going to come through this alive! It's a crime! I'm going to prosecute you . . . and I warn you . . ."

Mr. Brenske stepped into the corridor, but everything was quiet. Everybody was busily writing letters. But in one compartment, there sat—now stood, flanked by guards— the only undisciplined member of this group of twenty-one people who up to that time had behaved with such exemplary discipline.

"I'm not going to write you a single line, even if you carve me up alive," shrieked the livid Rappaport-Lieben, and Mr. Brenske nodded to the guards to open the doors to the other compartments. Now everybody could hear everything; Mr. Rappaport-Lieben was howling in a fury, but the others diligently went on writing their letters, leaving the telegram with its blood-curdling ransom fee until last.

"What have you got there in those buildings with the smokestacks?" cried Rappaport-Lieben. "What do those flames come from that blaze away, day and night? What weird kind of factories are they? What are those ovens toward which those silent streams of people were marching this morning? Who is tearing little children into pieces? And who's made beggars out of us and now doesn't even want our money anymore, but money from our families?

120

Next time it'll be money from our neighbors, then money from the people who live across the street and in other towns and from people all over the whole world. I can't stand this anymore. I won't stand for it! You might as well kill me too!"

"We really should have at least a chance to talk to someone in authority from the International Red Cross," Mr. Oscar Lowenstein whispered suddenly. "They ought to show some signs of interest themselves, I should think, or else we ought to remind them. Just a few words . . ."

He sounded more anxious than ever. There was an undertone of deep indignation and an even deeper sense of wrong.

Rappaport-Lieben stared around him like a man gone blind and then he began to shout again. "Why don't you get it over with right away? What're you waiting for? What International Red Cross? Whoever believes that one must have eyes made out of gold. I don't believe a thing by now. This is an expensive case of blackmail and murder. There's no law here anymore. The only thing that counts is death. . . ."

Perhaps there was a certain majesty about his howling, but none of the others heard it except Katerina Horovitzova.

Mr. Brenske glanced into a few of the compartments and he stood so Katerina Horovitzova could see how sorrowful he looked. But she didn't see his hand as it gestured to the guards to do their duty. It happened just as Rappaport-Lieben was yelling that the ship was a snare and a delusion and that nobody would ever get on board, because otherwise why was the train standing there for so long? Anyway, he didn't even believe in this train, he cried. When Rappaport-Lieben screamed that he'd known another kind of Germany and he hoped that after he was dead Germany would rise up and cleanse itself of this trash, saying the ones who were ruling the country now were criminals, Mr. Friedrich Brenske's eyelids quivered with distaste. The guards drew their pistols and shot Rappaport-Lieben.

Then there was silence and in a loud, clear voice so everyone could hear, Mr. Brenske told Herman Cohen, "I'm sorry this has happened. You saw for yourself that I didn't give any such order, that I didn't have a chance to do a thing. I was expecting he'd come to his senses. It was probably just a case of hysteria. Sometimes that happens when you've been under a lot of pressure of different kinds. I'm really awfully sorry about it. All right, have you got your letters and cables ready? I'd like to get going with this and move on toward the final solution."

The guards carried out Rappaport-Lieben's body and then people heard the doors slam shut in the last coach. When they came back, the guards brought along cold refreshments which apparently had been prepared in advance. They distributed the food. It was like a little banquet at some station restaurant—servings of roast stuffed pigeon and slices of cold turkey and duck, French and German-style salad, army-ration canned pâté, white rolls and dark army bread, along with cider and beer and white Moselle wine, depending on everybody's taste. The pigeons looked like roasted crow.

"I suggest you all have a little bit of refreshment," said Mr. Brenske. "I'm hungry myself by now."

With strange, slow reluctance, almost revulsion, everybody began to eat, particularly Mr. Schnurdreher and Mr. Varecky, who were in the rear compartments. The guards, most of whom had stayed at their posts, watched while their mouths watered.

They found no comfort in whatever feelings they may have had toward one another now, or in pride, or in their common destiny or the debits and credits they shared. They had suddenly had enough of it all and they were hungry and thirsty. Fastidiously, Mr. Klarfeld spread a white linen napkin over his knees. Mr. Otto Rauchenberg did not eat a bite or drink a drop. They looked as though suddenly nothing mattered anymore. In the meantime, someone slammed the door of the train from outside.

Mr. Brenske gathered up the letters, anxious lest the envelopes get greasy. They were nice letters, even though they were a bit shorter than he had expected, and written by trembling hands. When the scribbling was too bad, he suggested that a P.S. be added to explain that the unsteady handwriting was the fault of the moving train. Messrs. Adler, Schnurdreher and Lowenstein immediately complied and—although they couldn't see one another—their movements and gestures were practically the same. Mr. Freddy Klarfeld insisted on rewriting his letter.

"We're going to wait for an answer from your families," Mr. Brenske said wearily. "In the meantime, enjoy your view of the ship and your supper. This will be your last meal as our guests. I hope for the time being we aren't in anybody's way here on this wharf." Suddenly, without anybody having noticed how it happened, the flags of the German Reich and the United States, which hung like sisters, had slipped to half mast.

The guards from Katerina Horovitzova's and Herman Cohen's compartment, who had carried out Rappaport-Lieben and brought back the food, returned to their places.

Before anyone realized it was they, someone in one of the other compartments remarked that the customs officers were on their way. This remark was passed on from one compartment to the next in different variations.

"Isn't that a handsome ship?" Mr. Brenske asked Katerina Horovitzova, who was feeling chilly. She turned up the collar of her fur coat, almost hiding her glossy hair, and she agreed.

"Even though it may be wrong to bow down to things or people," Mr. Brenske went on, "this ship really merits it."

"It's very beautiful. I still can't imagine how we're going to feel when we'll be on board and waving good-bye," Mr. Cohen said softly.

Mr. Brenske chuckled. "Very well put."

"Are we really waiting for the customs officers?" asked Mr. Cohen.

"No, we won't bother you with such details. After all, you don't have any secrets from us. Or do you?"

He left without saying where he was going or when he was coming back.

"Maybe he's talking to the man from the International Red Cross," said Mr. Lowenstein loudly enough for his neighbors to hear it in their compartments on either side, the way prisoners talk to each other through the walls.

"One of us ought to be present."

They were waiting for cabled replies and their spirits drooped because by now their bank accounts were empty.

But there were still their families' bank accounts. Beyond the window, the ship rocked gently, glittering like a queen against the blue-gray sky with its name, *Deutschland,* visible on the stern and prow.

All was silent on board the ship. Evidently the crew had

not yet been given orders to get ready to sail. Cranes loomed behind the ship. This was the quietest part of the wharf. It didn't even look as though there was a war going on, at least not from the train. It was a pleasant view, but there was a great deal of inchoate melancholy about it too.

Mr. Brenske came back three hours later. "The mail left long ago," he said. Then, visibly impatient, he added, "Well, it doesn't look as though either your families or your authorities are burning with desire to see you again. The exchange has hit a snag on your side. We've noticed this same kind of indifference toward the whole operation on the part of official circles in your country right from the start. It's as though in your country too they apparently think more of your bank accounts than they do of you yourselves . . . and also some of our military figures; but I don't want to be tactless. Whoever digs a trap for someone else usually falls into it himself. . . . Don't count your chickens before they hatch. But this round hasn't been won yet. Obviously, in some respects, war and a feeling of enmity don't spare even an operation like this exchange. Apparently your relatives can't put their feelings ahead of business. Or can they? It looks as though even the International Red Cross is helpless here. Miss Horovitzova hasn't been put into Mr. Herman Cohen's passport yet, either. But I'm not losing hope about this or anything else. I've already arranged for an alternative solution."

"What do you mean by that?" asked Herman Cohen.

"I won't keep any secrets from you. Right now we're forced to pay for this ship and make up for everything that's already been invested. It's too bad, but that's not all. On orders of our higher authorities, I'm canceling the sailing because willingness to negotiate on the part of the other side (I don't mean you personally, but of course this affects all of you, directly and indirectly) has remained at the freezing point."

At an unseen gesture from Mr. Brenske, the guards drew the blackout curtains so that the ship, which everyone had been obediently watching as Mr. Brenske had suggested, suddenly disappeared from view. Katerina Horovitzova thought about Rappaport-Lieben and then she remembered Rabbi Dajem from Lodz and the tailor too. The sea roared. It sounded as though it was a long, long distance from the wharf. It was only then that she could visualize her family, her grandfather, Father, Mother and all her sisters including little Lea, and recapture scraps of memories about things that happened when she was a child.

"Now what's going to happen?" Mr. Cohen asked slowly. "Does this mean we've been deceived?" His voice trembled.

"I hold the International Red Cross responsible," said Oscar Lowenstein. "I want a chance to make this point."

"Was it a lie? Has all this been just a lie?"

"Not in the least," replied Mr. Friedrich Brenske, looking Mr. Cohen straight in the eye. "Not in the least, I repeat. This simply means we're changing our plans. We aren't masters of this situation ourselves. Actually, we'd expected at least as much cooperation from others of your faith, if not quick action and nobility of spirit, as has already been shown by our side. And even your side. I'm not speaking of the authorities, because they are institutions, if I may say so, and institutions are impersonal in a way. It would be foolish to wait around here for sympathy and understanding. It simply hasn't been forthcoming. Those who have

their freedom don't realize as well as you do what's important and what isn't. Those who have plenty to eat don't
believe those who are hungry. But we won't give up yet.
Then, too, canceling the sailing means there's still enough
money left in your accounts to get you to Switzerland and
you can look out for yourselves after that. I've left a certain
amount of money aside for such an eventuality. We're
really going to have to let somebody else take care of you
from now on. Unfortunately, this is dragging on for too
long. And we've all got other worries. On both sides. You
can probably understand yourselves what kind of worries I
have in mind. All I'm afraid of is the resentment which
some of you may feel just now and that's why I'm not even
going to go into detail about these worries of ours. Also,
I don't know whether I'll be able to go all the way with you,
but I'll try my best. I want to see this thing through to the
end, like a responsible and honorable man. So now what I
want you all to do is to write another letter in which you
explain in detail where your people are supposed to wait for
you. Write them that there's a delay of several hours. I don't
think it'll take much longer than that. Just a matter of hours.
We'll start on our way immediately. All we'll do is change
our route and who knows, maybe it'll be all for the best,
with the sea as rough as it is today. And as far as the
representative is concerned who's arranging this whole
thing, I spoke to him when I went outside the first time. I
don't think his authority goes so far that we ought to overes-
timate his importance. He simply isn't as influential as we
wish he were."

"What do you mean by that?" Herman Cohen asked
again, even more quietly.

"I've already explained it to you," replied Mr. Brenske.

"There are some people among us here," demurred Herman Cohen, "who find it hard to believe you by now."

Mr. Brenske thought awhile, hesitated and finally said quite frankly, "Then that's their fault, not mine."

"Why did you shoot Mr. Rappaport-Lieben?" asked Freddy Klarfeld suddenly. "After all, we're prisoners of war. Everything's been handled so conscientiously: the receipts, the money. . . . Mr. Rappaport-Lieben will be missing in your calculations."

"Yes, he will," admitted Mr. Brenske. "It shouldn't have happened and I admit it and I'm trying to explain it too. Some of the guards are extremely sensitive about their race and about the orders of our supreme leaders, sometimes even more so than these leaders are themselves. In other words, not all my countrymen have this idea of *noblesse oblige* in their blood and the strength, or rather the ability to endure and forgive insults against the Reich. That's not surprising. These are just simple people. Brute force is alien to us, but you usually get what you ask for. I may find this regrettable, but there's nothing I can do to change it. This is war, so consider Mr. Rappaport-Lieben as a casualty of war. After all, under the conditions in which we're living, he might have caught typhus or scarlet fever or got an infected liver, for instance, through no fault of yours; he could have stepped on an unexploded land mine, been hit by shrapnel or inhaled poison gas. I've even mentioned this possibility, I believe. You've got to count on casualties on our side as well as on yours."

In a few minutes the letters were written.

"Will they get there in time?" asked Herman Cohen.

"I hope so. You must trust me," replied Mr. Brenske.

128

"We're in your hands and we expect you to do what you promised and what we've paid for."

"Certainly, certainly," said Mr. Brenske absently. "I don't think anyone living in this country—that is, not a single person could be found within the latitudes and longitudes of our globe who would say this wasn't so. Everything will turn out just as we said it would. The final solution is at hand. You'll see for yourselves. Your worries will all go up in smoke and burn away like brush fire. From my own personal experience, I can testify that people often don't believe things which concern them in the most fundamental way until they feel them on their own skin. It's really very interesting. But there I go, I've wandered off the subject again and everybody is always primarily interested in his own affairs. We mustn't let ourselves get depressed. We want to liquidate this exchange operation in the best possible way. You must listen to what I'm telling you. Until we've reached a destination which will be satisfactory to everybody and about which you'll have no fault to find, I'm doing my level best to make this trip as pleasant as possible for each and every one of you. I'm sure you won't mind if I go with you right to the end of the line. But without discipline, it will all be much more difficult."

"What's going to happen with Mr. Rappaport-Lieben?" asked Mr. Leo Rubin.

"As far as Rappaport-Lieben is concerned, as much as I regret it, I must tell you what I told you about Mr. Cohen's marriage to Miss Horovitzova," said Mr. Brenske. "The laws of our Reich simply do not allow Rappaport-Lieben to be buried on our soil. That's another reason why—in addition to your disinfection—we will have to stop at some camp on our way to Switzerland. It's really not as far out of our way as you might think. I've got in mind the nearest one, but if it isn't practical or possible to stop there, then we'll go back to the mother camp. We'd have to do this anyway, even if it weren't for Rappaport-Lieben, because the Swiss authorities insist that you be disinfected. I already mentioned this to you, so we'll just be killing two birds with one stone. We're obliged to abide by this regulation. Switzerland is not part of the Reich. Yes, but first Rappaport-Lieben will be properly buried so you'll feel better about it. I'll see to it myself that he gets a proper funeral. Someday perhaps those who have died here will get just the same sort of treatment as unknown soldiers. We'll put flowers here on the anniversary of their death. Well, that's about all for the time being. We won't be asking you for any more money. Everything's been paid for and we're all even. Gentlemen, I hope you won't lose patience. I urge you not to and I suggest it earnestly. Before night falls, you may possibly be in Switzerland already. But it depends on you too."

Mr. Brenske then started to leave, but he turned back.

"Your situation would be easier if you'd write a few more letters. For one thing, it helps to pass the time and for another, it may soften up our superiors, who are considerably disturbed by the callousness of your relatives on account of the ship. And for the rest of the time, why not take a nap so you'll feel fresh and rested? Is anybody hungry or thirsty? Does anybody need medical attention?"

For a long time, the train stood beside the wharf. Then another locomotive was attached, a steam engine from the sound of it. This reminded Katerina Horovitzova of the black smoke at the place to which she was returning. Finally the train began to move and they traveled for seven long hours without a single stop, each person under guard in his own compartment.

THREE

WHEN THEY GOT to the mother camp, Mr. Friedrich Brenske excused himself, disappeared into the German administration building and came out a little while later, dressed in a new gray-green uniform and cap. He was freshly shaved and he even looked as though he had taken a bath. Everybody from the train had gathered in a small area in front of an underground dressing room which had double wooden doors. There was barbed wire all around them, of course. The doors looked very solid.

Mr. Brenske addressed them. "In order for us to be able, within the time we've indicated in the cable we've sent ahead, to exchange you for our prisoners—and we hope they will be the ones we want, the ones who are important to us—we must have you disinfected, as you know. Vaccinations against typhus and diphtheria won't be necessary because you were not taken prisoner in the field but in the hinterland, and there are different regulations which apply to that. Of course, I don't rule out the possibility that the Swiss themselves might vaccinate you later. They're very fussy about these things and you may have to spend a couple of hours in quarantine over on their side. Here it is essential that your clothes be disinfected and that you take a bath. But that's certainly not so terrible. I mention it simply so you know what's going on and so nobody can accuse me of neglecting something for the good of the cause. Beyond those double doors, as you see yourselves, is the dressing room. We have no unnecessary secrets. Unfortunately, there is no separate dressing room for ladies. I wasn't able to arrange for one in such a short time. I couldn't even have found anybody to do it. The exit is on the other side. This is all just knocked together, sort of, on account of the war. It's not much, architecturally speaking, as you see your-selves. It's all very simple here. Field conditions must be maintained.

"Gentlemen, up to now you have shown—those of you who are standing here now—an exemplary self-discipline and you have nothing to be ashamed of. I've already had dealings with many of your people and I wish they would all have had your good judgment and your patience. This patience has been, is and will continue to be the fundamen-tal condition for the success of this operation. Don't pay any attention to certain discomforts. I must ask you that person-ally. I admit and I've made it quite clear that this isn't a place full of a lot of unnecessary luxuries, even for us. And I'd like to point out to you once more that we're back on camp territory again. For this reason it is essential—for you and for us—to abide absolutely by all orders, because regula-tions are sacred here. So I want you to listen carefully to what I have to say to you now. Take off your shoes, remem-ber the number of your clothes hook and when you come back through the hall from the other side, go right back to your own belongings without any more reminders. In order to avoid any confusion which might delay us later, put your passports, money and other valuables in the cupboards under the hangers. You'll get everything back from the guards after you've had your bath. I ask you not to talk to any of the local personnel."

Mr. Brenske planted his feet apart and coughed dryly.

"I've had a cold buffet lunch prepared for you later, so there will be absolutely nothing to delay us anymore. Also, I've just found out that a Swiss physician will be going with us the rest of the way. He is at the same time also an official of the International Red Cross. The airplane bringing this doctor is just landing at the local airport." Then, with a small, almost vacant smile, he added, "They say all's well that ends well."

Suddenly, he was no longer able to look the gentlemen straight in the eye. But he did his best. The guards surrounded them just as thickly as in the synagogue earlier. Everybody was used to it by now and paid no attention. In a way, the underground dressing room and bath resembled the synagogue where they had been before and, by coincidence, this occurred to both Mr. Cohen and Mr. Rauchenberg, who couldn't see very well without his glasses. Perhaps it was also because of the tense way Mr. Brenske looked. He probably thought so too. Apparently he had not lost patience or interest in them, even though his involvement had dragged on for a long time as things became increasingly complicated. Maybe he was looking forward to a rest during their trip. Now, for the first time, they noticed that outside the underground dressing room, behind the cordon of guards in their frog-green uniforms, stood a group of men in prison clothes. For a moment Herman

Cohen even thought he recognized the tailor among them. Mr. Brenske, standing even more straddle-legged than before, seemed to be waiting for them to obey his orders. His expression was graver now and slightly sour, probably because nobody moved to do what he had told them.

"Is it really necessary to go through with this disinfection?" asked Mr. Herman Cohen. "You said we'll be in Switzerland in the morning."

"It's still morning. Not later than seven o'clock. Switzerland is a little bit closer than Hamburg. It'll certainly still be morning by the time we're ready to leave. We'll reach our destination as fast as we can. The sooner we start, the sooner we're finished. I repeat, it all depends on how much discipline you show now. This is no time to quibble over details. I said 'in the morning' and it is morning." Mr. Brenske's voice was mild but he was getting angry. Now he seemed to bite off his words, or perhaps it was because he was in uniform. He spoke very brusquely, as though the whole thing made him suffer. They really might have a little pity for him, his piercing eyes told them. He wasn't made of steel, after all.

"You can't go on straining my good will and my patience," he said. "I don't behave that way with you. I'm sure nobody's pampered our prisoners over on your side. You've got to take a bath. We weren't the ones who thought that up; the people who are expecting you did. From the bottom of my heart, I loathe telling anyone they *must* do something—particularly people like you. I know people of your kind would rather make up their minds by themselves. A little bit of hygiene never hurt anybody, though, and the very first thing I did when we got back here was to go into the barracks and have a hot bath and shower.

You can't imagine how that picks a person up. Sometimes a bath like that is all we've got left to do. Well, now, enough of that. . . . In the meantime, we'd better have your clothes pressed. You mustn't go away looking all mussed up. Now I'm going to make the final arrangements. While I'm doing that, get yourselves in shape as I told you. Don't act like naughty children. It's your life, not mine."

Suddenly Mr. Vaksman stepped forward and said, "I'd like to point out that—as far as my racial origin is concerned—I have documents to show that I'm not completely . . ." He didn't even have to go on and tell to what degree he was of mixed blood.

"I'm sorry," Mr. Brenske interrupted, as though he had immediately understood what Mr. Vaksman was trying to say. "These things are not decided either by you or by me—I mean, at this particular moment. . . ." Again he smiled that quick, vague, almost vacant smile which seemed to say that in the end, what a person is or isn't is not determined by his actual origin or any kind of conclusions which might protect even a victim, but simply and exclusively by him and people like him. His eyes spoke and they said: Dear friend, be good enough to let us judge whether or not you are what we want you to be. We know how to do our job by now. We aren't the first in such a situation and we certainly won't be the last.

Mr. Vaksman looked around him searchingly and there was more understanding and amazement than curiosity in the eyes which met his. Everything that Mr. Brenske had said so verbosely could be summed up in one of his favorite proverbs: if someone wants to beat a dog, he can always find the stick to do it with.

Then Mr. Brenske turned and left without another word.

Mr. Lowenstein didn't get a chance to tell him he'd like to see the absent intermediary with his own eyes. Somehow it didn't seem to have much point anymore. They watched Mr. Brenske leave and they noticed at the same time that more soldiers had entered from the other side. At an order of a lieutenant, the men in prison clothes approached and gave everybody a little cake of soap. By coincidence, Katerina Horovitzova was given her soap by the tailor with the ashen eyes. Now they looked even grayer and more opaque.

"We meet again," she said.

"Yes," the tailor said, nodding. "Everybody gets his just reward."

Not another word was spoken.

Mr. Vaksman kept staring at the floor. That was when he realized that one's race and what one belongs to are never determined by the race itself, but by those who have made these concepts a necessity and use them as a shield. Otherwise it would not make any sense. And he wondered what his colleagues would say if he told them this.

All nineteen gentlemen suddenly seemed oblivious to the fact that they were not alone. Without any more reminders, they moved toward the dressing room as though they had forgotten that Katerina Horovitzova was there and that she was a woman. Perhaps it was because they'd been given the soap, or the atmosphere of the underground dressing room, or Mr. Friedrich Brenske's speech, his promise that a Swiss doctor would be going with them the rest of the way; or perhaps it was because of the feeling of insecurity they had when Mr. Brenske finished his speech and left them, for in a way they had got used to him. They felt orphaned in his absence. Or maybe it was the shower room itself and all those guards and the strange lieutenant and, finally, the fact that they wanted to get it over with. But Katerina Horovitzova did not take off her clothes.

The underground dressing room resembled a garage, with a sloping cement floor down which they moved toward the benches and the numbered clothes hooks. The men in the striped prison clothes had disappeared again behind the wall in the back and the guards moved closer. Now they stood among soldiers whose uniforms were a different, brighter shade of green and up in front stood the new lieutenant. The soldiers' faces were impassive for the most part and if anyone had wanted to describe what was most striking about them, it would have been this very impassivity. They smelled of mothballs and ersatz cloth and something like shoe polish. Except for the open pistol holsters, everything about them was neat and tidy. At first glance, they looked as though they were on leave. Maybe it was also because many of them really were off duty. The lieutenant was softly whistling a German marching tune. He was substituting for Mr. Brenske, who had gone off to wind up their affairs.

Wearily and slowly, the holders of the American passports finally began to get undressed, exposing their white nakedness. The lieutenant prodded them with a thundering roar: "Come on, hurry it up, gentlemen, so you can get your bath and so the water doesn't get cold. Everything's ready for you over there behind that wall and through the doors in front of you. All you've got to do is get started."

And then he added in an even rougher tone than he had perhaps intended, "Now, gentlemen, nobody's got any special privileges around here as far as taking your time is concerned. Everybody—young, old, women and children

—they've all got to get undressed in a hurry. There are others waiting. You wouldn't want them to have to wait on account of you."

Evidently this was a speech he'd often made, because now, of course, there were no children. But while Mr. Brenske had always spoken persuasively, the sharper tone seemed more appropriate and effective here, although the lieutenant added that privileges might be waiting for them once they got into the Swiss Alps somewhere. Here, however, they must keep in step with army regulations, he said. The men who had come in in their bright green uniforms chuckled at that. This apparently encouraged the lieutenant, who began to laugh even louder than the rest.

"Put your passports in these cupboards here. You'll get back all your papers and junk when you get to Switzerland."

The guards could all see that none of the naked gentlemen wanted to part with their passports, but obviously they couldn't take them with them into the bath. So finally they had to leave them. It took Mr. Walter Taubenstock the longest to do so, as might have been expected.

"Well, you are a nice little spoiled brat," the lieutenant told him. "I'd like to have you in my hands for a while. I'd teach you differently. Have they always handled you with kid gloves, or what? You've been spoiled rotten. Switzerland's not going to help you any. What you don't learn now, you never will."

Whenever he said "Switzerland," the lieutenant rocked back and forth on his heels as though he himself didn't believe very much in its existence.

Katerina Horovitzova watched how all the nineteen men, including Herman Cohen, slowly filled the shelves with all

142

their belongings, first placing their American passports carefully on the bottom and laying over them their watches, tie pins, gold cuff links and spectacles, all the while murmuring words of encouragement to one another. Mr. Walter Taubenstock was the last to do so. She saw them, one after the other, pulling off their wedding rings and the other rings they wore, while the men in uniform kept on laughing. Mr. Freddy Klarfeld put everything neatly in its place. It was a pleasure to watch how meticulous he was, as though the tidiness of his belongings really mattered.

The members of the special crew who worked in the underground dressing room stood motionless behind the wall in the back, ready, perhaps, to pass out towels or to be useful in some way. The tailor was there too. Mr. Cohen hadn't been mistaken after all. They were quiet as mice. The men in uniform—like the prisoners—seemed to be looking intently at these men's shoulders, which Katerina Horovitzova could not understand. Otherwise she thought she probably understood everything now. She was not worried by the reluctant scurry of her fellow passengers. She looked around but still she did not get undressed. She observed everyone who watched her, waiting for her to begin, particularly the lieutenant who was substituting for Mr. Friedrich Brenske. She puzzled over what the tailor was doing here and then she remembered how Mr. Brenske's eyes had flashed when he had referred to the message she had sent out in the suitcase and how frightened the tailor had been and how he had hunched his shoulders. The other nineteen in her group, scared by the shouting and laughter, began to take off their underwear and put it on the shelves piece by piece, until she turned away from them so she couldn't see.

"Here nobody needs to feel embarrassed for the way he was born," the lieutenant said roughly. "And especially not in front of us. If you only knew what a parade of nudes we've already seen here!"

The guards chuckled again; they'd been looking forward to the fun while these Americans had been traveling back and forth in the train, while they were admiring the handsome, freshly painted ship, and while they were diligently writing letters after they could no longer contribute from their own bank accounts to increase those of Mr. Brenske and his superiors.

"Hey, sweetheart, don't tell me you're really embarrassed in front of us?" asked a young guard who was standing behind the lieutenant. He probably meant it seriously. The others laughed at him, particularly the lieutenant.

"Right!" goaded a second guard up in front. "What's embarrassing about the way a person's born?"

"Get back, kid," the lieutenant shouted at the younger guard. It was Lieutenant Horst Schillinger. He was the one to whom Mr. Brenske had given his instructions when he had gone to change his clothes at first and to whom he sometimes passed on some of his observations and advice, as the judicial branch passes on its recommendations to the executive. He was about forty years old and he looked like a killer.

"Now watch how you handle a flock of sheep that won't behave," he said, and began to shout, "Take off your pants, gentlemen! *Dali, dali!*"

This was a German expression which everybody understood. It meant do it fast. In an instant, all nineteen men stood there naked. They held their hands in front of them

144

like substitute fig leaves and because they were really cold.

Sly chuckles were heard.

Katerina Horovitzova blushed slightly, but she simply lowered her eyes. She heard and saw nothing of what was happening. These were no longer men in any of the senses in which she had defined men to herself before. She didn't look at anyone in any of the three groups—not at the nineteen naked men, or the ones in uniform, or those in prison clothes. The embarrassment she felt was of another sort and it was turned against herself.

Maybe she had simply forgotten to get undressed as she stood there thinking over what had happened to them during the last few hours, but she looked defiant in her fur coat when everybody else was either naked or stiffly buttoned up in uniform. She might have been able to stay that way for quite a long time, lost in thought, recalling years gone by, in her life and in others' too. But she found a different outlet for the feverish excitement and embarrassment which filled her.

"Hey, now, doesn't that go for you too, you cute little kike?"

And the lieutenant asked, "Say, where did you dance with those gorgeous legs of yours? We've heard a lot about you. Aw, come on, tell us. Let's see, huh?"

Up until that moment, there had been something of the child in Katerina Horovitzova's face, but whoever knew how to read a person's eyes would suddenly have found maturity and understanding there. She waited to hear what the lieutenant would say next. She didn't have to wait long.

"Well, *dali, dali,* take off those beautiful rags of yours," he prodded her. "Strip off everything you've got on your body. Anyway, all the stuff came from here. Go on, take off what you've got underneath too. This is probably the last you'll see of it. No use making such a fuss."

Without looking into her eyes, which glittered not only with comprehension but with hatred too, he explained, "We know what's going on, all of us you see here hanging around and wasting our precious time this way. We've been around and we've seen plenty. It's a fact, they're waiting for you down there in Switzerland, up on some mountaintop, most likely, where the air's first class. But they want you clean as a lily, so you can't get out of taking a bath."

With his last words, he took pity on her and became serious. He stepped closer as though he wanted to help her off with the fur coat.

But just then Katerina Horovitzova began to take off the coat herself, probably so the lieutenant would not touch her.

She let the fur coat slip from her shoulders and down her back. She glanced around the room and because the clothes hooks were on the other side, she let the coat fall to the floor. Lieutenant Schillinger watched her closely and when it was obvious that she intended to continue, he stepped back so the others could watch. She had been successful with the initial effect she had wanted to achieve. Her fingers toyed with the buttons on her blouse and skirt, while she watched him contemptuously, with no more trace of a stubborn child's capriciousness. Her glance swept over the men in uniform who stood in front of her, but it did not touch for a flicker of a second those in prison clothes or the naked ones. Her eyes were the color of old honey, glowing with a weary defiance. She was no longer frightened by what the lieutenant had said to her. She didn't believe a word of it,

and if she was still afraid, for the first time in her life she
succeeded in overcoming fear. She smiled to herself at the
way she had watched that big beautiful ship, the *Deutschland.* She had probably stared at its strong steel prow for
longer than any of the others. They had allowed them to
gaze, she thought to herself now; it was worth it for them
to go to such expense, just to put more money in their own
pockets. They had extorted huge sums of Swiss gold right
from under the noses of these nineteen Americans. She
could not appreciate the value of so much money. Some of
the naked men there in the dressing room were watching
her reproachfully because she was holding things up. They
probably still didn't realize what this was all about. But she
knew by now—she knew everything, or almost everything.
She wondered why the tailor was there. This had surprised
her. She belonged here, on the other hand. There was no
getting away from it. The camp was everywhere. She had
her race and her origin and there was no escaping them.
Suddenly she wondered whether there really was any other
world beyond this camp. Her fingers dropped from the
buttons on her blouse and skirt. It was obvious to everyone
that she was not going to get undressed now, if indeed she
had ever intended to when she had removed the fur coat.
All the men in uniform were properly dressed, even snugly,
and they couldn't catch cold like the naked men who stood
there, huddled together to keep warm. There was no
longer any difference between those who had American
passports and those at the other end of the underground
washroom in their zebra-striped clothing. Mr. Landau and
Mr. Klarfeld nervously inspected their white bars of soap,
which were about the size of matchboxes. Freddy Klarfeld
memorized the factory number stamped into the side of the

soap as though it were a matter of commercial importance. It must be a pretty cheap brand of soap, he thought to himself. Katerina Horovitzova realized she wouldn't be able to keep on her clothes much longer and she stared at the floor. Lieutenant Horst Schillinger hesitated for a minute, but encouraged by the way she had averted her eyes, he shouted at her suddenly.

"Well, what's wrong?" It sounded much better in German. *"Was ist denn los!"* As though he were herding cattle.

But it wasn't necessary to translate it, or most of what he said after that, and fortunately this didn't even occur to Mr. Herman Cohen. He had even forgotten about the debits and credits filed away with Mr. Friedrich Brenske and perhaps he'd forgotten everything else too. His soft white hands, which he held in front of him, were trembling, and this affected the other eighteen gentlemen.

Katerina Horovitzova could feel the debility which emanated from the huddle of human beings there beside her as they shivered in the raw autumnal air. She wasn't embarrassed any longer, as the men in uniform thought she was. She had stopped getting undressed for quite a different reason. She understood everything that had happened during these last few hours and she did not think about what was to happen in the years ahead. There were no longer any years ahead. Only a blind man could believe there was still hope. For a moment she could still see the huge, apparently unsinkable ship, the *Deutschland,* and hear the roar of the sea and the rattle of the Pullman coach wheels as they rushed along the rails. She stepped sideways so she wouldn't fall if Horst Schillinger or someone else stuck the muzzle of his pistol into her ribs. She imagined she heard Mr. Friedrich Brenske's voice.

"Get undressed," Lieutenant Schillinger said. "You made a pretty good start. What're you stalling for now? Got your soap? You have? Did we give you the number of your clothes hook? Sure. We've done our part; now get a move on and don't hold things up!"

And to emphasize his words, he put his hand on his pistol butt.

She noticed his gesture without the slightest fear now, prepared for anything.

"What's holding up your stockings? Is that the main holdup?" He chortled, pleased with his wit. "Come on, come on, do what you're told! Get those clothes off. *Dali, dali, dali!*"

He saw that now his orders would be obeyed. He grinned complacently. People almost always obeyed him.

(Later, Mr. Brenske told Lieutenant Schillinger's platoon that "if we assume our enemy's character is like a fortress we must storm in order to grind him into dust, then we must also assume that this fortress has its weak points. But we mustn't ever be too sure of ourselves. When you're looking for examples, I might compare the walls and its loopholes to a tiny door which has been overlooked in the fortifications of what was once the most important city in the world when it was conquered and yet it was a city on which its would-be conquerers broke their teeth." Mr. Brenske could feel how much vital experience breathed from this sentence, experience few people before him had ever had. He savored all its many meanings and he had no more to say, even though, in other circumstances, he was never chary with words.)

Everybody's attention was fixed on Katerina Horovit-zova now. She lifted her skirt, revealing smooth white legs from her thighs down past her knees and to her ankles; she slipped off her shoes and left them lying next to the fur coat. Horst Schillinger gulped, without even realizing that during the past twenty-four hours many German men who had been responsible for her or who had been in her presence had done the same. He didn't have to remind himself about the other women he had had or about his own Hildegard, because all that was quite different. And unconsciously he gulped again, lecherously, enviously and appreciatively. He was entranced and he did not conceal it in front of any of the other men. Katerina Horovitzova didn't have to be urged anymore. She no longer seemed to be paying any heed to what was going on around her. With a slow deliberateness that grew out of something somewhere inside of her, she took off the skirt with its five buttons, which had been made for her not long ago, then the black silk blouse. She didn't even bother to take her clothes over to the hook; she simply let them fall to the floor. Nobody said a word.

"What do you say about that, kid?" Lieutenant Schillinger addressed his young deputy hoarsely. "Take a look at the handiwork of the Jew god."

Now Lieutenant Schillinger decided he would make her take off her last garment. His lips were moist, as though he had been drinking. Suddenly he cursed her coarsely.

"What're you so scared of, you Jew Carmen?"

And he added something even worse, which almost gave the game away to the huddled bunch of nineteen naked men.

This was the cliff, the chasm which they had been approaching for a long time; but its dimensions had been adjusted in their own minds to fit their hopes. Up until just a little while ago.

A lot of words had been kneaded into different shapes in order to make this self-deception easier for them and a great deal of effort had been invested. This in itself may be looked at in different lights. These people had been transported to the brink of the chasm, to the edge of the cliff, accompanied by debits and credits and Wagons Lits. They could hear the rustle of the leaves in their bankbooks as a great ship rocked at anchor and words were spoken to them, assuring them that life can be bought and death be paid off. Now preparations were being made to give it the form of a bath and an empty shower. It was no longer so easy to tell oneself that there was a lake on the other side of the chasm or beyond the cliff and that if a few chosen people had enough strength and the opportunity, they could swim to safety on the other side. There was only the great, gaping pit, nothing more. They could see it now, right in front of them. Mr. Leo Rubin began to say his prayers. Mr. Rauchenberg squinted and Mr. Cohen fixed his gaze on the girl's head and on her expression, which was sterner and more austere than it had ever been before. He foundered in the brown and green depths of her eyes. They were infinitely deep.

Lieutenant Schillinger cursed again. It was the worst curse Katerina Horovitzova had ever heard and he wound up by ordering her, "Take off those rags! You're going to dance for us like we tell you to!"

He said a lot more, but there is no need to repeat it. She touched her underclothes.

"Don't worry," Horst Schillinger encouraged her. "Every well brought up lady takes her sunbaths naked at this swimming pool."

This touched off even louder laughter. That is probably

why he added, more for the others' sake than hers, "Rent your underwear from our company. Fully guaranteed. Use our brand."

She had to lean slightly backward to unfasten her brassiere. She bent her arm sharply at the elbow and suddenly ripped off the delicately embroidered piece of white lingerie, striking Horst Schillinger right between the eyes with the hooks at the end of it, just as he was laughing hardest. He was momentarily blinded by surprise as well as pain. Hundreds of thousands of people had already passed through this dressing room, as docile as sheep, and nothing like this had ever happened before.

Lieutenant Schillinger couldn't react, either with amazement or by fighting back. He had been entirely unprepared for the blow he had been struck. Eyes blinded by stinging tears, he could feel Katerina Horovitzova yanking the pistol out of his open holster. It felt as though it were happening far away. He groped for the gun but it was gone and she shot him in the stomach. He crumpled to the floor with a wolfish howl. His deputy, the young man he'd just called "kid," had his wits about him and jumped forward. German soldiers have always been trained in a spirit of close comradeship and no one had ever undermined this moral character of theirs. Almost at the same moment, another shot flashed from the muzzle of the pistol in Katerina Horovitzova's hand. It was only a tiny flicker in comparison to all those belching chimneys and, unlike them, it soon went out. But the kid's body crumpled too. She could feel her heart beat, but she had heard nothing. Not even the dry crack of the bullet. She simply understood and killed. And it wasn't at all as impossible as it had seemed all her life or even at the moment she was pulling the trigger. Now the other

152

Germans swiftly drew their pistols, but some of them didn't have time. Others fumbled and dropped their guns in the shuffle which followed. All of them, without firing a shot, moved back to the first door so they would not injure their own men, so they could keep their backs covered and so that the naked group which was shifting uneasily from one foot to the other could not escape. But it hadn't even occurred to the nineteen men to try. Two young soldiers held the unarmed herd at bay while two of their uniformed comrades carried out the wounded. They were followed by the rest of the soldiers. They were probably afraid that Katerina Horovitzova might fire another shot. All that stayed behind was a stretcher which one of the retreating platoon had shoved in from outside like a taunt. And the nineteen men. Mr. Leo Rubin was still saying his prayers.

Suddenly Mr. Friedrich Brenske's frosty voice sounded from the back of the dressing room.

"Now, now, what's all this, gentlemen? It would be a tragedy if you aren't able to get going in time. Everything's arranged and your diplomatic representative will have a word with you after you've had your bath. Everyone I've spoken to is waiting for you by now. The Swiss physician is just outside—a Red Cross official. Gentlemen, for goodness' sake, calm down."

His voice, without any trace of excitement, echoed with all the other things he'd told them between the two sundowns. It had a hollow ring to it, as though it were coming from a great distance. Perhaps he was trying to control himself so he could speak calmly—or speak at all.

He was answered by another pistol shot from Katerina Horovitzova, whom he had overlooked in his appeal. She fired, but it didn't hit anybody because she didn't really know how to aim the gun. With each shot she fired, she said somebody's name. The last was Lea's.

Mr. Brenske spoke up again, but this time not to the chosen people with American passports. "Commandos, get busy!" It sounded reluctant.

Then several men in prison clothes rushed out from around the corner of the wall where they had been crouching to protect themselves from ricocheting bullets. The tailor was among them. They snatched up the weapons which had been dropped, but they didn't turn them toward where Mr. Brenske stood. Instead, as he intended when he shouted his command, they aimed the guns at the nineteen men and one woman who stood huddled together. They herded them all into the washroom, after which a man in prison clothes slammed the outer door and secured it with an iron bolt. The tailor wearily rested his skinny hand against the bolt, and for a second he closed his eyes as Mr. Rauchenberg had been doing. He understood a lot; there was a lot he didn't understand and there was a lot which had been inevitable. When Lieutenant Schillinger had at first questioned whether the tailor should be present at all, Mr. Brenske had explained that "when a lion tamer shows any weakness in front of an animal, he's finished." Then, too, Mr. Brenske and Lieutenant Schillinger had realized for some time that blood and blood relationships alone are never decisive, even though German professional magazines were full of that very thing just then. It was strength that counted, rather, and the realization of which side has the superiority and power and who will be the one to present the bill when the rebellion is over. For Lieutenant Schillinger, the exception had simply proved the rule. Reward played its role here too. So the whole thing, like everything which had happened before and that which came after, really took only a few seconds.

Katerina Horovitzova was closest to the door and she could feel Herman Cohen's cold body behind her. At first, she beat against the door with the pistol butt and then she used her fists until her knuckles began to bleed. While the light was on, she could see how the room looked inside. Mr. Samuel Landau and Mr. Freddy Klarfeld were clutching their soap as if they didn't want to part with it for the life of them. There was a blue light like a cellar bulb set deep into the rough concrete ceiling and covered with a rust-proof wire grille. The shower heads were pear-shaped and the dilapidated floor drains stank. The doors were tightly shut and nothing made sense anymore. She could feel the dampness, probably because people just like them and naked just as they were had taken showers here not long ago. She was wrong. The dampness had another cause. But they were the same kind of people.

"Those were our own people who herded us in here . . ." said Herman Cohen. There was a shocked astonishment in his voice. Then he added with much less surprise, "Rappaport-Lieben knew. Maybe we all knew, really." And then he said, "I smell gas."

Now he understood what the people had been whispering about on the ramp. Their "there" was *here*.

That was the only time Katerina Horovitzova almost screamed, but just as she opened her mouth, she almost strangled on her own saliva. It was all she could do not to choke. After that, she was quiet, but she began to beat against the door, which was made of good strong German oak. Mr. Schnurdreher was losing his senses, because first he said that Mr. Rappaport-Lieben had saved himself from this and then he corrected himself and said he'd brought it on himself. With Mr. Klarfeld's shoe, which had somehow found its way into the washroom, he began to hammer at the light bulb in the ceiling, destroying their only source of light. Nobody even tried to stop him. Katerina Horovitzova's pounding on the door gradually grew feebler too.

They were in darkness.

After a few minutes, the doors opened suddenly and the blinding glow of a flamethrower drove the little throng into the farthest corner of the room.

Suddenly Katerina Horovitzova's grip loosened and the pistol she had been holding slipped from her fingers to the floor.

Mr. Friedrich Brenske and a dozen men in frog uniforms, wearing helmets and armed to the teeth, set up their machine guns in the doorway of the washroom. The Jewish commando crew stood behind, the ash-eyed tailor among them. Without much fuss and at the command of Mr. Brenske, they began to mow down the twenty people, one by one. Mr. Brenske didn't even try to deliver one of his grandiloquent prologues. He didn't say anything anymore about how nice it would be if both sides joined forces against their most deadly enemy, as he had made a point of doing so pertinently before. He didn't bother with any eloquent oratory. It wasn't a part of the program and it wouldn't have been appropriate anymore.

"Fire," he said again. "Now it's your turn. . . ."

Mr. Brenske had accepted without objection the request of Lieutenant Schillinger's platoon that it be handled this way and with these weapons. It was neither a wise idea nor a foolish one; it was simply following the precept "An eye

156

for an eye and a tooth for a tooth," as one of the soldiers said.

Mr. Hans Adler was the first to be shot, as though things must always be done alphabetically. Then Johann Ginsburg and Stepan Gerstl were executed, almost together with Oldrich Ekstein. Herman Cohen came next. He had been trying so hard to convince himself of his own manliness that he had not even thought to pick up one of the loaded pistols which had been dropped in the melee. Then it was Katerina Horovitzova's turn. Thanks to the perfection of German weaponry, it was all over in a second. Even the clack of the machine guns and the ping of the empty gilt cartridges were soon over. Those who had been manning the guns crouched there for a second and then they all got up together.

Slowly a few of the men entered the washroom, along with Friedrich Brenske, followed by the prisoners from the commando crew. Among them was the tailor with the ashen eyes, who moved with noticeable listlessness. He had been assigned to the crew as a punishment by Mr. Brenske, because of the message for Katerina Horovitzova's family which had been found in the bottom of the suitcase in which he had brought the lingerie to the synagogue. That was scarcely twenty-four hours ago, counting last night. The tailor had known what his daily duties were going to be from now on and he knew that his days were numbered too. The Chief of Cremation made no secret of this to any of them. The men in Lieutenant Schillinger's depleted platoon finished off the last two moaning survivors, short-sighted Mr. Otto Rauchenberg from New York City and Mr. Sol Raven from Los Angeles, originally from Warsaw. German military language has an apt and much-used word for this: *Genickschuss*—the *coup de grâce*.

Mr. Jiri Vaksman and Messrs. Josef Varecky and Benedict Zweig lay across one another as though someone had stacked them up into a pyramid or for a campfire so all that was needed was to strike a match. The others were scattered around on the floor like logs.

Mr. Lowenstein's mouth was half open as though he had wanted to ask for something at the last minute.

Mr. Friedrich Brenske, the specialist for this group of twenty with their genuine American passports, went into the washroom because he was conscientious. He wanted to find Katerina Horovitzova. He said to himself, All I do is step out for a little while and all sorts of things begin to happen. Well, here I am, back again, so everything's going to be all right.

The men in uniform kept on shouting at one another excitedly and bumping into the commando crew in their striped clothing.

The tailor leaned against the wall like a pillar of salt. Katerina Horovitzova was lying to one side of Herman Cohen, who had always been right up front as the intermediary and interpreter (though he wasn't always absolutely accurate), whose word carried the most weight between Mr. Brenske and the side which his own officials so inadequately represented. But if he could have done so, Mr. Brenske might have comforted Mr. Cohen now and told him that long before he and his American friends had come on the scene—and long after they would have left—a lot of people more vigilant and less credulous than they had been had also been lured from the path of judgment and reason. Mr. Brenske was an expert at the job. Or perhaps he wouldn't have said anything like that after all, simply because their trip to the final solution had run so smoothly, until a little while ago, accompanied by illusions, which can be lovely things even if they're lies. Such illusions can escort their victims to heaven or hell to the accompaniment of the sweetest-sounding words.

What Katerina Horovitzova had done came as a real surprise to Mr. Brenske, even though nothing usually surprised him and he could have written a book about human credulity and what fear can make a person do. She had been killed by one clean shot right through the heart. The machine gun had behaved with tact and moderation. There was only a tiny, bloody-edged circle on Katerina Horovitzova's soft and strikingly white breast, a spot which of itself —or perhaps because of the resilience of her young skin— had drawn inward as though it wanted to hide. Mr. Brenske gave orders that her body should be left here for the time being while the others could be burned in the usual way. And then he commended the Jews from the commando crew who had helped the men in uniform in such an exemplary way, as though they had been bound in an invisible comradeship to those who killed against those who were killed. As a reward, they were to receive larger food rations tomorrow and for the next three days. Each of them would also get a can of blood-streaked horse liver pâté, a can of smoked fish from the German seas and a bottle of domestic rum. Then he ordered everybody to tidy things up so the next operation would not be delayed. Mr. Brenske smiled with dry contentment. He was rather tired, but he didn't let it show because he was still on duty. He knew how to reassure and comfort other people and that is why he had got as far as he had. Under different circumstances, he might have devoted himself to the occult, but even this assignment had its advantages as a temporary alternative. Actually, a momentous idea was taking shape in his mind at that very moment.

The next day, starting at sunrise, the body of the nineteen-year-old Jewish dancer Katerina Horovitzova was exhibited on the order of Mr. Friedrich Brenske in the warehouse next to the oven where hair was usually dried, hair which had been cut from the heads of dead women when they came out of the gas chambers. Everything had been thought of with meticulous care. Part of the commando crew hosed down the waxy bodies they had just removed from the gas chambers, to cleanse them of all undesirable discharges and excretions. This might be blood choked out of ailing lungs or it might be the normal blood of child-bearing women or young girls. Sometimes the blood had been drawn by its owner's fingernails or by someone who was standing close. Some groups included a great many children and it sometimes happened that a few of them survived because the bodies were packed in so tightly that the gas did not penetrate all the way down to the level of their heads.

As every informed person knew, this warehouse was the place where Rabbi Dajem of Lodz reigned. He never stopped saying his prayers, even when they finally brought in the body of Katerina Horovitzova and piled it on top of the others as if on a catafalque. He entwined himself with the religious articles which—for most people—bear unintelligible Hebrew names, and after that he gazed night and day at the person whose marriage service he had performed and who in death still had all her hair, which was as beautiful as silk. It was black as coal. Sometimes, in moments of clarity, which were like something between a sunrise and a sunset, Rabbi Dajem from Lodz compared it with the souls of his jailers. He was not allowed to die because once, when he had begun to sing in the transport group which was going to the gas chambers, Mr. Friedrich Brenske had heard him. He picked him out and let him live. After that, Mr. Brenske kept insisting to him that they must be friends because comradeship is never impossible, no matter how improbable it might seem. He assigned him to sing to the dead women's hair until it was dry and ready to be shipped off to Germany, where it would be used for making nets and mattresses and cloth. Suddenly the place was full of rats. Surely there were more of them than there had ever been before. They weren't even afraid of people.

For three days, from dawn to sunset, the camp directors came to look, at the invitation of Mr. Friedrich Brenske. First the officers came from the camp and from the secret division, then noncommissioned officers, and finally the enlisted men. After everybody else had come and gone, some of the Jewish prisoners were permitted, or rather commanded to come. The tailor provided the commentary about what had happened. At first, when the officers came and hence there were fewer visitors than later, Mr. Brenske asked him whether he could make a few adjustments on the suit he had made for Herman Cohen so that Mr. Brenske could wear it himself. It had looked so nice when they left for Hamburg. And he also asked him to find another fur coat for his wife, Gerda, just like the one he'd got in the warehouse for Katerina Horovitzova. A little bigger through the shoulders and around the waist, though. She was coming to visit him during winter vacation.

"Yes, sir," said the tailor respectfully.

But after that, Mr. Brenske ignored him. The tailor didn't look quite so benumbed anymore, just preoccupied. He felt as though he would be able to do anything now; a condemned man finally puts his own head in the noose because even when he stands under the gallows, he is willing to believe, if someone persuades him in the right way, that sulfur and fire are sugar and cream and that he'll be able to enjoy them to his heart's content after they send him away to where he doesn't know a soul. Naturally, they would execute him without a qualm because the dead can no longer testify against themselves to show they were mistaken. At most, he might still be able to shed a few tears while still alive, either with the rope under his chin or else with the first whiff of gas in his lungs. Because it never should have turned out this way. But until that time, why shouldn't he make himself useful?

Mr. Brenske was daydreaming; he thought about the tailor, the fur coat for his wife and about a thousand other things, most of them different from the others. Each such thought was like a very minor sin and all these banal offenses and omissions had their own built-in rebuttal.

In his report submitted somewhat later to headquarters in Berlin, Friedrich Brenske described in detail the case of this group which had been captured in Italy after July 9, 1943, had held American passports until the end and had been so grossly rejected by their own authorities (at least from the administrative aspect). As though the worth of German generals and high-ranking officers could not be measured in gold! He told how he had undertaken an exhausting—but, from his point of view, successful—train trip to Hamburg, thereby gaining additional valuable experience, as well as a tidy additional sum for the German

Reichsbank. He mentioned Katerina Horovitzova's mutiny, making a point of her beauty and her expression of almost childlike innocence, using this as the excuse for the death and wounding of members of the secret division, particularly the late Lieutenant Horst Schillinger and young Sepp Hoyer, known as "the kid" among the other men in the platoon, who had been shot while he was trying to take the pistol away from her. He wrote about the danger which had faced all twelve men who might have been seriously injured and he mentioned that Sepp Hoyer would probably remain a cripple all his life. But at the end, he noted the amount of money which this operation had brought in. To this he affixed a period and his signature. (With all his experience and erudition, Mr. Brenske had no idea that his story of Katerina Horovitzova would remind his superior in Berlin of another woman, who had cut off the head of a certain general. Of course, she'd got him good and drunk beforehand. So it was no surprise that Mr. Brenske didn't refer to it in his report. Even so, it made a fascinating story.)

Mr. Friedrich Brenske glanced over his work. It looked very nice. In the meantime, his adjutant had opened the window and from the nearby drying room he could hear Rabbi Dajem from Lodz. He was singing. His song was awfully melancholy, but undeniably beautiful all the same. Thoughtfully Mr. Brenske smiled to himself and said, "For them it's natural and for us it's madness. Or is it the other way around?"

But he didn't answer his own question.

And Rabbi Dajem from Lodz began to caress Katerina Horovitzova's hair as he had once before. Then he stroked her cheek. As he did this, he spoke to her. "Ah, my little one, ah, my gentle little one. My brave child. May your name be blessed, even before God's own name. You courageous little one, my fighting spirit. May your name be blessed a hundred times."

And later he watched how her body burned, after the hair had been cut off. He said it all once more in his song, which neither Mr. Friedrich Brenske nor his adjutant nor any of the others understood.

"... A hundred times courageous, a hundred times good, a thousand times just, a thousand times beautiful," he sang.